⌐•THE GREAT•⌐
SHELBY HOLMES
AND THE COLDEST CASE

Also by Elizabeth Eulberg
The Great Shelby Holmes
The Great Shelby Holmes Meets Her Match

THE GREAT
SHELBY HOLMES
AND THE COLDEST CASE

ELIZABETH EULBERG

illustrated by **ERWIN MADRID**

BLOOMSBURY
CHILDREN'S BOOKS
NEW YORK LONDON OXFORD NEW DELHI SYDNEY

BLOOMSBURY CHILDREN'S BOOKS
Bloomsbury Publishing Inc., part of Bloomsbury Publishing Plc
1385 Broadway, New York, NY 10018

BLOOMSBURY, BLOOMSBURY CHILDREN'S BOOKS, and the Diana logo
are trademarks of Bloomsbury Publishing Plc

First published in the United States of America in September 2018
by Bloomsbury Children's Books

Bloomsbury books may be purchased for business or promotional use.
For information on bulk purchases please contact Macmillan Corporate and
Premium Sales Department at specialmarkets@macmillan.com

Library of Congress Cataloging-in-Publication Data
Names: Eulberg, Elizabeth, author.
Title: The great Shelby Holmes and the coldest case / by Elizabeth Eulberg.
Description: New York : Bloomsbury, 2018.
Summary: Unexpected media attention in their Harlem neighborhood brings Shelby Holmes,
nine, and John Watson, eleven, a new case that sends them undercover as figure skaters.
Identifiers: LCCN 2017056224
ISBN 978-1-68119-057-0 (hardcover) • ISBN 978-1-68119-058-7 (e-book)
Subjects: | CYAC: Mystery and detective stories. | Friendship—Fiction. | Ice skating—Fiction.
| Undercover operations—Fiction. | Ciphers—Fiction. | Harlem (New York, N.Y.)—Fiction.
Classification: LCC PZ7.E8685 Gs 2018 | DDC [Fic]—dc23
LC record available at https://lccn.loc.gov/2017056224

Book design by Jeanette Levy
Typeset by Westchester Publishing Services
Printed and bound in the U.S.A. by Berryville Graphics Inc., Berryville, Virginia
2 4 6 8 10 9 7 5 3 1

All papers used by Bloomsbury Publishing Plc are natural, recyclable products made from wood
grown in well-managed forests. The manufacturing processes conform to the environmental
regulations of the country of origin.

To find out more about our authors and books
visit www.bloomsbury.com and sign up for our newsletters.

For Beth Eller and Courtney Griffin,
who have been amazing cheerleaders for Shelby, Watson, and me.
(Let's hope it doesn't go to Shelby's head.)

CHAPTER
1

SOMETHING WAS WRONG WITH SHELBY HOLMES.

You couldn't really say she was in a bad mood since her usual mood was ah . . . sour. But it was clear there was something going on and it wasn't good. I practically had to jog to keep up with her after school on Monday. She was muttering under her breath.

"Everything okay, Shelby?" I asked.

Her reply was a grunt.

Okay, *that* was a typical response from her. Next, I would attempt to do what Shelby always did: not simply see, but observe. I would put all the detective skills she had taught me to use and figure out what was going on.

This was what I'd noticed so far: she was her usually prickly self on the way to school. Nothing new there. It was really at lunch when things changed. She sat by herself at her regular table. However, instead of eating, she folded her arms and glared at her lunch bag. After that, she slammed her locker door between classes, and people cleared the way for her more than usual. She didn't speak at all in science class, and her agitated behavior continued on our walk home.

It had to be something that happened with her lunch. She normally spent lunch period with her head crammed into a book and devouring an assortment of desserts. She didn't want to "waste precious research time" talking to her friends. Well, her *friend*. Singular. Since she only had one and that honor went to yours truly.

Shelby kept speed walking as we went farther away from the Harlem brownstone where we both lived. "What happened with your lunch?"

Shelby abruptly ended her power walk to turn to face me. "Lunch?"

"Yeah, you seemed upset with your lunch."

"Go on." She looked impressed.

Wait. This must've meant that I was onto something. Soon I'd be like Shelby, deducing a person's life story with a single glance!

"Where are you going right now?"

"To Kristos." Kristos is a deli in our neighborhood, where Shelby liked to get her sugar fix.

No way. It couldn't be.

The pieces of the puzzle started to come together. Shelby being really angry. Her not eating lunch.

I couldn't believe it. The impossible had finally happened.

And if my deduction was correct, we were all going to suffer for it.

"Your parents aren't letting you have any sugar."

Shelby's pale face turned the same color as her bright red hair. Between clenched teeth, she said, "Yes, my parents voiced their *objection* over the amount of sweets I'd been consuming. And they decided to share their *concern* with every purveyor of sweets in the neighborhood."

So here was the thing: Shelby's parents were completely right. Not like I'd ever admit that to Shelby. The girl *inhaled* sugar. And not like a cookie here or there. Several candy bars or cookies at once. Sometimes I didn't think she even breathed between bites. Candy was her preferred payment method when we solved a case.

"If you can't buy candy, I can get you some." While Shelby really should cut back on her sweets, I wasn't going to be the one to deny her candy. I valued my life too much.

Shelby tilted her head. "Think, Watson."

"Ah, I can handle buying candy. I'm around you enough when you eat it." It didn't really bother me that Shelby constantly ate sugar around me. Now, if she did that with pizza and didn't share, we'd have a problem. Anyway, it seemed pretty simple to me: Shelby's parents have told people she couldn't buy sugar, but that didn't mean— "Oh."

"Exactly," Shelby replied, knowing I figured it out.

If I went into Kristos to buy candy, they'd know it was for Shelby since I'm not only Shelby's friend, I'm also diabetic. Therefore, the ban affected me as well.

(Shelby needed to start giving her parents more credit for how smart they were.)

"What are you going to do?" I asked.

Shelby walked right up to a woman on the street corner who was waiting for the light to change. She got onto her hands and knees, examining the woman's boots.

"Can I help you?" the woman asked Shelby. She was probably in her midthirties and dressed in a jacket and skirt.

"You really should only walk on the sidewalk. The street can be a very dangerous place to stroll," Shelby stated as she stood back up and wiped her hands on her baggy jeans.

Where was Shelby going with this?

"Okaaay," the woman replied before turning her attention back to the stoplight.

Shelby continued, "While the construction on 128th Street can be a bit of a nuisance, you should've crossed over to use the sidewalk on the other side. But I understand it was more convenient to walk on the road. If you crossed over, you'd have to do it yet again to turn on Frederick Douglass."

The woman glanced back at Shelby, her eyes wide. "What? How did you . . . Have you been following me?"

I couldn't help but smile. I loved when Shelby did this. How she could seemingly pull information out of thin air so easily. But it wasn't easy. It was deductive reasoning.

"No, I wasn't following you," Shelby replied with a smile. "It was quite simple, and I can explain if you would be so helpful as to go into that store and purchase me a candy bar. I'll even give you the money."

The woman stepped back for a moment to get a better look at Shelby with her messy hair and Harlem Academy of the Arts maroon polo shirt. The corners of the woman's lips curled. "Okay, you've got me interested. I'll play along."

The woman waved away Shelby's money and in a couple minutes came back with a chocolate bar. Shelby tried to grab it, but the woman held it up high. "I believe you owe me an explanation first."

"Happily," Shelby remarked before dropping back down to her knees. She pointed at the woman's right boot. "You have a fine dusting of dirt on the right side of your right boot, but nothing on your left boot, which indicates that you recently walked by dirt that was to your right. Since we are predominantly surrounded by concrete pavement in Harlem, there aren't a lot of places in the general vicinity that you could've come in contact with dirt, except the construction that has blocked half the sidewalk on 128th Street. Most people would've crossed over, unless you were planning on taking the next right, which was Frederick Douglass."

The woman looked down at her boot. "But it's so . . . simple."

It was, but Shelby was the only person who could put it all together.

"Yes. It's also correct," Shelby stated as she held out her hand. The woman laughed as she gave her the chocolate before crossing the street.

Shelby ripped open the wrapper and wistfully finished off the candy bar in four bites. She had a spring in her step as we made our way back home. But once we turned the corner onto Baker Street, Shelby let out another exasperated sigh.

"What is it?"

Shelby glared at me. "That"—she pointed to a woman standing outside our apartment building—"is all your fault."

ᓚ·CHAPTER·ᓓ
2

"WHAT DID *I* DO?"

Shelby shook her head as we studied the woman from the corner. "It's that online journal of yours."

I couldn't make the leap to figure out how a woman standing outside our building had anything to do with the journal I started about our cases. My online readership really only consisted of a few classmates, my parents, and my English teacher. Oh, yeah, and one Moira Hardy, AKA the only person to ever outsmart Shelby.

"She's a journalist," Shelby stated.

I examined the young Asian American woman writing in a spiral notebook.

Before I could even ask Shelby how she knew that, she started to explain. "She's taking notes outside of our building. There are only a few types of people who would do that. Mrs. Hudson has no intention of selling her brownstone. Therefore, we can automatically rule out real estate agents or building developers. Of course, detectives are observant creatures, but this woman isn't with the police. And you, Watson, should know the other type of people who observe and take notes."

"Writers," I answered as I thought of my own notebook in my backpack that I use to jot things down.

"Exactly," Shelby replied with a satisfied nod. "She is dressed in a business casual manner: nice jeans, blazer, not too much jewelry. So she's professional, most likely a journalist, but not someone on-camera. She has a large messenger bag, which no doubt contains a laptop."

"The bag could have other things," I argued. While I knew it was pointless to ever doubt Shelby, it was the only way I was going to learn.

Shelby raised her eyebrow. "Okay, I'll bet you twenty candy bars that she's a reporter. Or whatever the equivalent of twenty candy bars is to you."

No way was I taking that bet. I was curious, not a chump.

"How do you know there's a laptop?"

"Her left shoulder is lower than her right, signaling that she is carrying a lot of weight from her bag. My conclusion is that she has a laptop. Not only that, but she is here to interview us about your blog for her community newspaper, although with the current state of printed papers, I deduce that she writes for an online outlet."

"Really? She wants to interview us?"

Visions of fame floated through my head. My online readership would grow! I'd win awards! I'd be invited to go on television to talk about fighting crime!

"We certainly will *not* be participating in any kind of interview," Shelby said, extinguishing my dreams.

"Why not?" I whined.

Shelby scowled. "I will not be traipsed around the press as some *pint-sized detective* and hear *oh, isn't that just adorable*. No, our work should be taken seriously."

Okay, Watson. This was going to be a challenge to convince Shelby. I wanted to be interviewed so more people could see my writing. All I had to do was to get Shelby to say yes. And the best way to get Shelby to be agreeable (when chocolate wasn't around) was to feed her ego.

"Nobody could take what you do as anything but impressive, Shelby."

Her scowl softened slightly. "Well, you and I are aware of that fact."

"Of course. But wouldn't it be beneficial for people to know what a great detective you are? It would increase your profile, and once people read about how brilliant your skills of deduction are, we'll be flooded with more clients. Because, really, why go to the police, when you could go to Shelby Holmes?"

(Yeah, I was going a little overboard, but Shelby looked thoughtful at what I was saying.)

"You have brought up a good point, Watson." She paused for a moment. "Maybe."

Maybe! I was getting somewhere. Now I needed to turn that maybe into a yes. And I knew exactly how to close this deal.

"And just imagine how annoyed Detective Lestrade would be when she read the article."

Shelby brightened up. "You know what? A little press would be good for us. It would get more people to read your journal as well."

"Oh, yeah, I didn't think of that." (And seriously, the fact that I didn't crack up right then and there showed how much better I was getting with acting. Real undercover work was just around the corner. I could feel it.)

"All right, let's go," Shelby announced as we approached the woman.

The reporter was too wrapped up in writing in her notebook to see us coming.

Shelby cleared her throat. When the reporter looked up, she broke into a huge grin. "Oh, isn't this just adorable."

Before Shelby could insult the reporter, I reached my hand out to her. "John Watson, nice to meet you."

She shook my hand, while her eyes remained on Shelby. "Nice to meet you, John."

Shelby started walking up the stairs to the front door of our brownstone.

I gestured for her to follow Shelby. "We should go inside."

The reporter looked surprised. "But you don't know who I am and why I'm here."

Shelby turned around. "Yes, we do." She crossed her arms with an annoyed expression on her face. "Apparently you underestimate what Watson's been reporting about me. But I can verify that it's all true. And then some."

The reporter hesitated for a minute before she followed Shelby up the stairs with me trailing behind her.

Soon she would realize what a genius Shelby was (and that I wasn't such a slouch, either), and if we were lucky, a lot more people would want to put Shelby Holmes and John Watson on the case.

⌐•CHAPTER•⌐
3

"DID MY FAMOUS SON GET ENOUGH BREAKFAST?" MOM asked two days later as she poured herself another cup of coffee.

"Yes. I didn't realize notoriety could make you so hungry," I joked as I finished off the last of the scrambled eggs.

I scrolled through the article Lynn Chan had written in the Harlem Observer, a community blog, about Shelby and me called "Harlem's Smallest Sleuths." It was pretty good, even with that title. It talked about how we were able

to find the Lacys' missing dog and how we helped our science teacher, Mr. Crosby. It even mentioned a few of the cases we've cracked for our classmates.

I hadn't had a chance to talk to Shelby about it yet, but I was sure she'd have a ton of objections, especially to the fact that she was described as "adorable," and yes, "pint-sized." But at least she wasn't referred to as a "sidekick." That stung a bit. Sure, I didn't know as many random facts as Shelby, but I was getting a lot better with deciphering clues and deductive reasoning.

Also, it would've been nice if they had run a picture of us where I wasn't in the background. But maybe it was because the photo they did use for the article—featuring Shelby on the steps of our brownstone with her arms folded and an impatient grimace, while I was three steps up—was the only one where she wasn't overtly glaring at the camera. I had thought Shelby would've liked the attention that came with being interviewed and having her picture taken.

I had thought wrong.

Mom looked over my shoulder and read from the piece, "While they are small in stature, Shelby Holmes and John Watson can match wits with any detective twice their size." She patted me on the back. "My son, the media sensation."

Well, I didn't know about *that*, but it felt nice to get credit for what we've done.

"Did you send it to your father?" Mom asked.

"Yeah." I'd told Dad about it last night during our nightly phone call. I hadn't seen him since we moved over two months ago. He was supposed to come and visit soon, but he hadn't mentioned it in a while. I knew I'd be seeing him next month for Thanksgiving, but that was too far away.

"That's great," Mom said as she rubbed my hand. "I know you miss him, but you'll see him soon enough."

I guess. But it was a little unsettling that I'd become used to him not being around.

"Plus," Mom said with a smile, most likely trying to change the topic to a happier subject. "I bet this article will get you guys even more cases now."

(See, I was getting better at reading body language. That and I knew my mom really well. She could sense when I was down about the divorce.)

"Yeah, I hope so."

Complaints about the article aside (as I knew Shelby would have plenty), it would probably help us get cases from people beyond our school and neighborhood.

At this point, I wanted a case from anybody. Shelby was very particular with what kind of cases she felt were "worthy" of her talents. We hadn't had one in over a week. And while that doesn't seem like a lot of time, I was itching to get back to it. I was getting better with each case. Soon, I'd be able to solve something all on my own! (Okay, maybe I shouldn't get too far ahead of myself.)

"Now don't forget our rules."

"I promise I won't," I replied. "No more secrets."

Mom and I had an agreement when it came to working with Shelby: I had to tell her about the cases, and she needed to know where I was at all times. And I had to be extra careful with my diabetes and not go too long without eating or hydrating. Which totally made sense, but see, I kind of, sort of wasn't 100 percent truthful to Mom when I started working with Shelby.

Okay, okay. I had lied to Mom.

And yeah, I almost died that one time.

Oops. My bad. (For real, my bad.)

But now Mom knew everything. It was nice to be able to share our cases with her. I didn't like lying and keeping something from her that meant so much to me. Now during dinner I'd entertain her with tales of working with Shelby. Usually, she would shake her head in disbelief over something Shelby had done or said. Which, honestly, was how most people reacted to Shelby's talents. And attitude.

"Well," Mom said as she took her plate to the sink, "don't let all this fame go to your head. You still have to do the dishes."

"I don't know," I said as I put sunglasses on even though I was inside. "I might be too busy with my adoring public. You know how the paparazzi can be."

Mom laughed as she took off my sunglasses. While I did,

in fact, start doing the dishes. I knew my place. And Mom was never going to let me forget it.

There was a knock on the door, signaling that Shelby was ready to leave for school.

"Time to go," Mom stated as she took the dish towel from me. "Are you ready for your close-up, Mr. Watson?" she asked with a wink.

I opened up the door to a scowling Shelby. "Told you." She turned her back to me as she started down the stairs muttering, "Pint-sized. I'll show her what a pint-sized person can do . . ."

Well, it looked like it was going to be one of those days.

And I couldn't wait.

So, it seemed that my fellow classmates at the Harlem Academy of the Arts didn't read the Harlem Observer.

Although, I didn't really know what I was expecting. But today was like any other day. Except my buddies were really proud of me.

"You do realize that your writing is going to blow up," Jason said as we headed out of school. "Your journal is going to go viral. Just remember us lowly writers when the *New York Times* calls."

"I'm sorry, do I know you?" I taunted him. "You look familiar, but I just can't seem to place your name."

Jason let out his loud, infectious laugh. "Nice to know you won't forget where you come from, man. Hey, you up for some ball later? Got to get in as much time as we can before it gets too cold."

"Or we could play inside?" I argued. It was the middle of October and it was starting to get chilly. I didn't think there would be such a difference between the temperatures in New York compared to my old army post in Maryland, but this is the farthest north I ever lived. And it was cold. I shoved my hands into my pockets.

"Okay, okay." Jason pulled his long locs back into a ponytail. "We got to toughen you up. Also, you should know there's this stuff that comes out of the sky. It's called snow."

"Wow," I replied with fake awe. "Really? Nature, man."

Jason and I walked out of the school building to find Shelby standing on the corner, waiting for me. "I'll give you a call later," I told Jason before catching up to Shelby.

"Hey."

"Hello," she said as she unwrapped a candy bar. "You know, Watson, you were right."

I stopped dead in my tracks. Shelby rarely ever admitted that anybody, besides her, was right.

"About what?" I asked, and then made a mental note to mark this date on my calendar. It was a pretty momentous occasion.

"Friends," she stated as she shoved the chocolate bar into her mouth.

What? There was no way that Shelby could also be admitting that she needed a friend like me. I mean, what else could she mean. What had gotten into her? (Besides the sugar?)

She reached into her bag and got another candy bar. "Yes, having social acquaintances can be quite useful."

Wait a second.

"How have you gotten all those candy bars if both of us have been banned from buying candy?"

Shelby's lips curled in a smirk. "Would you care to make a deduction?"

She wouldn't. Would she?

Yes. Yes, she totally would.

"Shelby, did you make a friend so they would buy you candy?"

She shook her head. "Not technically accurate, but excellent deduction, Watson. I have made a pact with one of *your* friends."

"What! Who?"

No way would John Bryant get Shelby anything since she was his main competition in music class. I couldn't imagine him helping her, period. Jason hadn't said anything to me about it. Carlos was too intimidated by Shelby. That left . . .

"John Wu?"

"Yes! I discussed an arrangement with him in our acting class, and he was more than happy to oblige. I agreed to run lines for his upcoming audition for *Our Town* in exchange for him procuring candy on my behalf. This friend thing does have its benefits."

Gee, thanks, Shelby. I didn't want to explain that friends do things for each other because that's what friends do. But I wasn't going to argue since her arrangement with John would keep her stocked with sugar and therefore in a good mood.

As we turned the corner home, Shelby snorted. "Well, 221 Baker Street has become quite popular, hasn't it?"

There, outside our brownstone, was a white woman staring at the front door.

"Another journalist?" I asked. This was it! We were really going to become famous! Maybe it *was* the *New York Times*!

Shelby studied the stranger for a few beats before she pointed at her. "*That* is, once again, your doing."

"Oh, come on, what did *I* do this time?" And how come this stuff was always my fault?

Shelby cracked a smile. "No, this is a good thing, Watson. Let's go meet our new client."

CHAPTER 4

"WE HAVE A NEW CLIENT. REALLY?"

"What can you tell me about her?" Shelby asked as we
kept our distance from the woman.

"Wait. You don't know for sure if she's a client?"

Shelby glared at me. I should've known better than to
question her deductions.

Okay, let's see what I could figure out on my own. We
were still half a block away so I couldn't really examine her
that close. She was probably in her late forties, with black
hair pulled back in a tight bun. She was tall and thin, wearing
a red jacket and leggings. The back of her jacket had something embroidered on it.

Oh, no way. It couldn't be.

I squinted. "Are those the Olympic rings?"

"Yes."

We were going to work with an Olympic athlete? That
was so cool.

Best part: Shelby knew nothing about sports. I mean *nothing*. She referred to basketball as *the* basketball. She didn't think sports were "worthy" of any space in her brain attic. So if we were going to be working with an athlete, I would be the one with all the knowledge. I'd be truly indispensable.

It was about time!

"Let's go talk to her," Shelby said.

The woman saw us approaching and looked down at her phone. "You kids from article, no?" she asked with a heavy accent. "Detectives?"

Shelby reached out her hand and said . . . something. It sounded like gibberish, but the woman looked impressed and replied to Shelby in this foreign language.

She nodded again and then, mercifully, spoke in English. "So article is true."

I turned to Shelby. "What's going on? What were you—"

"I simply stated that she was from Russia in her mother language," Shelby clarified.

"You know Russian?" Come on! Where did she find the time?

"Of course! I feel it's imperative to study up on several languages. I began in first grade as it's best to learn languages when you're younger. I started with Latin since all the romance languages—Italian, French, Spanish, Portuguese—come from it. Then moved on to Russian and Chinese."

I mean, really. *REALLY*?

I was never going to catch up to her. NEVER.

"Let's focus on our new client," Shelby said as she turned to the woman.

The woman gave us a serious nod. "My name is Tatiana Pamchenko. I need help."

"Follow us to our office," Shelby stated as she began walking up the stairs.

Office? We had an *office*? Most of our clients came to us at school or we went to them. What was Shelby going to use as our office? The disaster area known as her bedroom?

"Watson," Shelby whispered as she opened the door for Tatiana. "We need to go to your apartment. Michael is home and will only be a hindrance to our efforts."

Michael was Shelby's older brother and, well, maybe not as smart as Shelby but with the same abrupt temperament.

I opened our apartment to Shelby and Tatiana. We filed into the kitchen.

Shelby tilted her head. "I must first state that sporting activities are not my expertise, but I deduce that you coach a sport that is in the cold."

"Yes, how you—" Tatiana began before Shelby cut her off.

"Your nose is a bit red and slightly peeling, which indicates that you wipe your nose a lot. While it could be a common cold, your jacket as well as your knit hat and gloves poking out of said jacket implies that you spend time in a cold environment. Additionally, your hair has a slight indentation where ear warmers would be. The weather outside, while cool, does not warrant those accoutrements. Especially for someone who grew up accustomed to frigid temperatures in Moscow."

"Impressive," Tatiana admitted. "I coach figure skating."

Figure skating? We finally got to work on sports and it was *figure skating.*

Ugh, life was so unfair.

"How can we be of assistance?" Shelby asked.

"Maybe it is nothing." Tatiana put her hand in her pocket.

"I'll be the judge of that," Shelby replied in her usual confident manner.

"Regionals are next weekend. It decides who goes to sectionals, then nationals. My star, Jordan Nelson, is beautiful skater. Such grace and consistency. She lands every jump. She is top of her field. But she got this yesterday and everything changed."

Tatiana pulled out a piece of paper from her jacket pocket and handed it to Shelby. On it were a few stick figure drawings that looked a little like figure skaters.

Shelby studied it closely while Tatiana continued, "After this, Jordan hesitate. No confidence. She missing jumps. I asked to tell me what means these drawings, but no answer. She no talk. There something wrong. I know her since she tiny child. She is like my own daughter."

Shelby stood up straighter. "Is this the only one you have?"

Tatiana nodded. "Maybe just silly drawings. But way Jordan acts, makes me think it is more."

"It's not a drawing," Shelby stated with the biggest smile I'd ever seen. "It's a cipher."

"What's a cipher?" I asked.

"It's a secret code," Shelby replied. "Each of these figures represents a letter. This says something. And Jordan can read it."

"I knew it," Tatiana said with a satisfied nod. "I thought police would not take seriously, but then I read story about you."

So it *was* because of me that she was here! Score one for Watson! (Although I knew absolutely zilch about figure skating and ciphers. *Sigh.*)

"Can you tell what it says?" I asked Shelby. While Shelby was smart, I had no idea how anybody could figure it out. All the figures looked alike. They only had a few small differences. A raised hand here, one foot up there. How anybody could read that was beyond me.

"No, but I presume it's a threat," Shelby replied.

"A threat?" Tatiana nervously wrung her hands. "Why you say this?"

"If it is affecting Jordan's skating, it certainly isn't about unicorns and rainbows," Shelby stated dryly.

Good point.

"Does she have any enemies?" Shelby asked.

"*Da*," Tatiana replied with a nod. "She is best skater. Many people jealous of her."

"I would like a list of people who interact with Jordan.

Anybody who would've been able to pass her this paper. Also, include individuals who could benefit from Jordan skating poorly. And anything you can think of that may help. I do mean anything. What may seem like a little matter to you may be significant to me. Understood?"

"*Da*," Tatiana said again. I was pretty sure that was Russian for yes.

"I'll need more data before I can crack the code." Shelby held up the paper. "Can I keep this?"

"*Da*. This is copy. Here is my info." Tatiana handed Shelby a card.

Shelby extended her hand to Tatiana. "Okay, I'll begin working on this, and I'll confirm a time for Watson and me to visit the skating rink and meet with Jordan. Rest assured, we will get to the bottom of this."

"Thank you," Tatiana said with a look of relief as she shook Shelby's hand. "Please be quick. Cannot let silly paper ruin hard work."

Shelby nodded. "Don't worry, Tatiana. Watson and I are on the case."

CHAPTER 5

"AH, WATSON, WHAT'S SHELBY DOING?" CARLOS ASKED
after school on Thursday.

Carlos, John Wu, Bryant, and I were hanging out near
my locker, but our attention was down the hallway where
Shelby was leaning against her locker, staring at a piece of
paper. She'd been doing it all day. I knew it was the cipher
that had her mesmerized. Well, mesmerized and really, really
frustrated.

Shelby had spent our entire lunch break writing furiously
in a notebook, then tearing out what she'd written and crum-
pling it up before starting over again. (Of course, she did
find a few minutes here and there to eat an entire bag of
cookies John Wu had slipped her this morning.) Shelby was
distracted by the cipher all through science class also. At one
point, Mr. Crosby called on Shelby and she looked up at him
blankly. Everybody in class was shocked. Shelby usually
answered a question before Crosby had a chance to ask it.

But this time, she had no response. She probably didn't even know what class she was in.

"She's studying something," I explained.

"When isn't Little Miss Perfect studying?" Bryant snapped with his eyes glaring at her.

"Or, you know, she could be in a sugar coma, *John*," I said to John Wu with a nudge of my elbow.

"Yeah, are you two friends now?" Bryant asked, his shaggy blond hair moving as he shook his head. "Is she going to start hanging out with us? Because you know I would *not* be cool with that. I have to deal with her in music class with her perfect violin playing and her smugness."

John Wu pushed up his wire-rimmed glasses. " 'Love all, trust a few, do wrong to none.' "

"What?" Bryant replied with a groan. "What does that even mean?"

"Ten bucks it's that Shakespeare guy," Carlos called out. He pointed to each of us. "Who wants to take that bet? Anyone? Anyone?"

"It *is* Shakespeare," Bryant admitted.

Carlos threw his hands up. "Dude! Wait until I have a chance to get a bet going before you prove I'm right. Come on!"

John turned toward Bryant and said, "What it means is that I don't want to get on anybody's bad side, *especially* Shelby Holmes's."

Oh, how right he was.

"Yeah, you really shouldn't let her get under your skin so much," I argued to Bryant. Believe me, I knew how easy that was for her to do, but Bryant needed to accept the fact that Shelby was the best violin player and smartest student in class and move on. We all have seemed to accept it. I mean, not like we had a choice.

"So should I start buying her sugar?" Carlos asked as he quickly stole a glance at Shelby. "What kind should I get her? And, more importantly, would it stop her from snorting in class when I get an answer wrong?"

"Probably not," I replied with a laugh. Shelby couldn't be bribed.

"YES!" Shelby screamed loudly as she slammed her locker door. She spun around so she was facing me. "Brace yourself, Watson," Shelby called down the hallway.

I pretty much got used to bracing myself whenever she spoke. I wonder—

Before I could even start to guess what she was going to do, she took off in a full sprint down the hallway.

And she was running straight at me.

"Shelby!" I cried out. "What on earth are you doing?"

The guys took cover, while I did just as Shelby instructed and braced myself, because Shelby Holmes barreled right into me. I took a few steps back from her impact, but luckily didn't get knocked over completely.

"Whoa," Carlos commented. "Someone get that girl on a football team stat."

"Don't let me move you," Shelby said as she then started pushing me from all sides.

"Shelby!" I said as I reached out and held her by the shoulders. "Stop."

She took a step back and looked me up and down. "Can you pick me up?"

"Ah, yes. And at this point I'm tempted to do just that and throw you in that garbage can over there," I replied with a scowl.

"Don't be so dramatic, Watson," Shelby said with a tsk. "I'm simply testing your balance."

"Couldn't you have chosen a different location to do that instead of the school hallway?"

I mean, really. For weeks I'd been enduring Shelby's quizzes and tests on everything from micro-facial expressions to fingerprint analysis. Now she wanted to test my balance. By tackling me. At school. In front of my friends and classmates.

"Hey, Shelby," Carlos said as he took another step away from her. "Quick question: What's your favorite candy? 'Cause I wouldn't want to get you something you don't like, and it's so not a big deal to do it. Like, do you offer protection of some kind? Is there a payment process we can discuss?"

She ignored Carlos and continued her focus on yours truly. A few times she would elbow me, but I remained dead still. I wasn't going to have her humiliate me. Well, any more than she already had.

After a couple more minutes, I finally had enough.

"Could you just—"

Shelby cut me off with a raised eyebrow. "You should be happy, Watson. You get your wish."

"What wish? I'm pretty sure I never wanted to be made a fool of in front of the whole school."

A smile spread on Shelby's face. "We're going undercover."

CHAPTER 6

IT WAS HAPPENING!

John Watson: secret agent.

Yeah, I kind of went undercover when we went to retrieve Mr. Crosby's watch, but this was different. I'd have time to prepare and fully become someone else.

I, John Watson, was going to be a man of mystery! I was going to be like James Bond and have cool gadgets! I was going to make a mission impossible, possible! I was going to . . .

"What is *that*?" I asked Shelby when I arrived at her bedroom after dinner that night.

"Rollerblades." She then placed a helmet and kneepads on her unmade bed. "I thought it best for you to start on the sidewalk before we move to the ice."

Why would . . .

Oh no. No. NO. NO. NO!

I was going undercover . . . as a figure skater?

Of course that was happening. *Of course it was.*

Shelby continued, "It's important when going under-cover to be as prepared as possible. We must know our alias inside and out. But this is a very special undercover mission as we are going to pose as a figure skating pairs couple."

"You're skating, too?" I asked. I'd never seen Shelby do anything remotely athletic, except run. Although she did study jujitsu. If she was going to be better than me at this, I was going to be really annoyed.

Couldn't I have one thing I could beat her at? ONE THING.

"Obviously I'm joining you," she replied as she showed me pictures of an ice-skating rink. "We need access to the ice rink where Jordan practices. That was where Jordan was given the note. There are only a handful of people who have access to the locker rooms and rink in the early morning as it's closed for private skating. There are two rinks at Chelsea Piers. One is reserved for Tatiana's clients, which now include us. We're going tomorrow after school to observe the space and meet Jordan. Then Monday morning comes the real test: interacting with the skaters who use the other rink. It just so happens that rink is used by Sergi Petrov and his clients."

"Who's Sergi Petrov?"

"Tatiana's former pairs skating partner . . . and ex-husband."

"Yikes." Well, it looked like we already had one suspect and we hadn't even arrived at the scene of the crime. An ex-partner *and* ex-husband? We should just arrest the guy now. Not like we arrested people or anything. But still.

"Exactly." Shelby gave a nod. "And since Jordan isn't talking to her trusted coach, we need to insert ourselves into the equation."

"Okay, so where are your Rollerblades?" I looked around her bedroom. All I could see, besides her usual mess, were weird mathematic equations with letters and numbers on a giant whiteboard up against one wall.

"I'm going to learn using this." She held up a giant physics book.

"Oh, come on, Shelby. You can't be serious?"

"Of course I'm serious, Watson. Physics is a very serious and scientific method. Figure skating is all about friction, momentum, Newton's third law, angular momentum . . ." She tilted her head when she could tell she'd completely lost me.

Now I didn't know that much about figure skating, but it wasn't about science. It was about trying to balance on a blade going over ice without falling down. And they jumped. And wore really frilly outfits.

This was going to be a disaster.

"See this equation?" Shelby asked as she pointed toward $I_1 w_1 = I_2 w_2$ on the whiteboard. "This is the equation for rotation. *I* represents rotational inertia around the spin axis, while—"

"English, please." I mean, *Come. On.* Did Shelby seriously expect me to know anything about physics? I was in sixth grade math and science. Physics was years away. Thankfully.

"Watch," Shelby said as she sat down in an office chair with wheels near her desk. She pushed it away and then started spinning around in a circle. She held her arms out. "Now as I pull my arms closer to my body, I'll move more rapidly." As soon as she adjusted her arms, she started spinning faster and faster.

"Cool," I replied. Hey, maybe physics wouldn't be so bad after all.

Shelby stuck her foot out to stop the chair while I walked over to the whiteboard. There was this other equation I couldn't even begin to describe. But since it had to do with Shelby, I figured it meant trouble. "What's this the equation for?"

"I'm trying to figure out the mechanics of the death spiral."

"The *what*?" I did *not* like the sound of that.

Shelby took out her laptop and showed me a video of a guy and a girl skating. And then the dude, holding the girl's hand, rotated her around him, but she was leaning back and nearly parallel to the ground. Her head was only inches from the ice. So it would be more dangerous for Shelby than me . . .

"Don't get any ideas," Shelby remarked dryly.

(Sometimes I swear she really could read minds.)

She paused the video on the two skaters as they took their bow at the end of the program, both smiling and holding hands. They looked like siblings: white, blond hair, blue eyes.

"That," Shelby said as she pointed to the girl, "is Jordan."

"Who's the guy? Her brother?"

"Douglas, her former partner."

"*Former* partner?"

"Yes." Shelby began pulling up articles about Jordan and Douglas. "They were one of the top junior pairs teams when Jordan left to become a solo skater."

"Whoa." Seemed like we might have another potential suspect.

"Exactly." A grin spread on Shelby's face. "Lots of suspects."

I scrolled through the images of Jordan and Douglas through the years. They'd been skating together since they were little. They looked so much alike. I kept looking at the photos of Jordan and Douglas on the top of the podium, and the other couples with them, always a step or two below.

"Ah, Shelby, I think we're missing a huge problem with this whole undercover figure skating pairs thing."

Shelby groaned. "We don't need to skate at an Olympic level, Watson. We need to simply *appear* as if we're pair skaters."

"Yeah, but that's the thing: there's no way anybody would buy me as a figure skater."

"Why not? You're a rather sporting person."

Did she really need me to spell it out for her?

"Name one black male figure skater."

"Well, I can't currently name any figure skater besides those involved in our case. Can you?"

Um, she had me there.

"We both have a lot of research to do to get ready. We need to know more about figure skating. Of course, we must be able to skate with some competence. And then there's our aliases."

Yes! I'd been waiting for this. Shelby always came up with undercover names really fast. I hadn't yet decided what my name was going to be. I was thinking Desmond Jenkins. Or . . .

Shelby went over to the whiteboard and flipped it around.

On it were the names Roberta Downey and Julian Law.

"Julian?" I groaned.

"I was contemplating giving you the name Jude."

"Jude? Julian? Who would call a guy that? Those aren't real names."

"I think John Lennon would disagree with you on that," she stated flatly as she turned her back to me. "There's no point in arguing—it's already been done."

"What do you mean, 'been done'? You signed us up for something?"

Shelby walked back over to her computer. "What will be the very first thing some of these extremely competitive figure skaters are going to do when we show up claiming to be these skaters?"

Oh, yeah, right. We were coming out of nowhere before a big competition.

I looked over at Shelby's computer. "The internet."

"Exactly." Shelby typed something and then handed her laptop to me. There under the search for "Roberta Downey and Julian Law" were articles about us placing in a few competitions in central New York State. When I clicked on one of the links, I actually let out a gasp at seeing photos of Shelby and me fill the screen. Us. On an ice-skating rink. Granted you couldn't see our entire bodies, but they looked real.

Had I been to an ice-skating rink with Shelby?

"How did . . ."

"A guy owed me," Shelby replied. Someone always owed Shelby something. But that still didn't explain how she got those photos of me.

"Hey!" I pointed to one image of me from a few years ago. It was part of an old Christmas card of me with my parents. "How did you get that photo?"

"From your apartment."

"Mom didn't mention you needed photos."

"Nobody was home."

Wait a second.

She wouldn't.

Of course she would! She's Shelby Holmes! She has no boundaries!

"Shelby, please do not tell me that you broke into our apartment."

Shelby shrugged like this was totally normal behavior. "I was on a tight deadline and required these essential pieces for our investigation. I didn't *steal* anything. You or your mother would've given me what I needed if you were home. I couldn't help it if you were both absent when I required your assistance. No need to throw a fit about it. Everything was put exactly where I left it. Now, moving on."

Unbelievable. I mean, truly, truly unbelievable.

(I really wanted to try out that death spiral now. Maybe if Shelby got dropped on her head she wouldn't think that *I* was the one being irrational.)

"Tonight, study up on skaters and skating lingo. That should pass us off tomorrow, then this weekend we need to work on our skating."

"Fine." I gave in. There was no reasoning with her. I put the Rollerblades on while I sat on her bed. I then carefully stood up. My legs wobbled a bit and my arms were flailing around before I finally found my center of gravity.

"We don't need to be experts, we simply need to try to not fall on our faces," Shelby said precisely as I lost my balance and fell forward.

Being a figure skater was easier said than done.

~CHAPTER~
7

My name is Julian Law. I am a figure skater. My partner is Roberta Downey.

My new details kept repeating in my head as Shelby and I took the subway down to Chelsea Piers after school on Friday. I'd heard of Chelsea Piers since it's this huge sports and entertainment complex in New York. I'd been waiting to finally go. Got to admit, never thought I'd be visiting it for the first time to go figure skating.

Shelby spent most of the ride with her head in her ginormous purple backpack. Once she finally sat up, I noticed that she had some makeup on and was somehow able to get her unruly hair in a bun. She had already changed out of her Harlem Academy clothing and into leggings and a fleece. Now, dressing like an athlete was something I knew about, but Shelby wasn't that impressed by my black nylon track pants and sweatshirt. We were not skating today (luckily!). Just talking. Not like I had any idea how I'd be able to skate by Monday. I couldn't go more than two feet in Rollerblades without falling down.

Once we got off the subway, we walked the four long city blocks to Chelsea Piers. We had to make our way through a parking garage to the elevators to take us up to the Sky Rink. As soon as the elevator doors opened, we were bombarded by noise. The reception desk, rentals, concession stand, and pro shop had lines of people.

"Over here," Shelby said as we made our way past the glass door.

There were two huge rinks side by side. Along the length of the rinks were benches for people to watch, while the opposite side overlooked the Hudson River and New Jersey. Above us were a bunch of championship banners that hung from huge green metal rafters. It was pretty cool. And by cool, I meant it was pretty awesome, but also freezing. Good thing I brought gloves. And a scarf.

One of the rinks was packed with skaters fumbling around. The other was empty, save for Tatiana and one other skater.

"That's Jordan."

Jordan was gliding seamlessly over the ice. Tatiana was skating beside her as she talked. Jordan nodded with a fierce look before gathering speed as she skated backward. She leaped in the air and twirled around for a few seconds—it was crazy. As her foot landed on the blade, she was off balance and fell.

Ouch.

Jordan got up and started skating even faster. Tatiana was trying to calm her down, but Jordan skated past her. She jumped again and fell.

How could one piece of paper mess with an athlete's head so much?

Tatiana noticed us hovering, but turned her focus back on Jordan. As I looked around the rink, I noticed that *everybody's* eyes were on Jordan. I couldn't blame them. Even with the falls, she was still the best skater in the room. Tatiana skated over to Jordan and put her arms around her. Tatiana leaned in and talked to her for a few seconds. Jordan nodded and forced a smile. Then they both skated toward us and exited the rink.

"We go to office and talk, yes?" Tatiana said to us as she attempted to clear a way for Jordan. There were people hovering trying to get pictures with her. A few even asked for Jordan's autograph.

(It was just hitting me that our new client was big time. Big Time.)

We headed into a hallway and went into a small office with two desks right next to each other. Photos of Jordan and Douglas, along with a couple other skaters, lined the wall.

"Too many people. This is why we practice when rink closed," Tatiana remarked once we were inside.

"But I need more practice. Clearly," Jordan replied as she sat down.

"You sit," Tatiana ordered us as Shelby extended her hand to Jordan.

"Roberta Downey and this is my partner, Julian Law. It's such a pleasure to meet you." Shelby used the high cooing voice she preferred for when she's undercover. Her eyes were wide and her usual scowl had been replaced with a warm smile.

"Hi, I'm Jordan." Jordan shook both of our hands. While

she put on a friendly demeanor, there was sadness in her eyes.

"Yes, we know," Shelby said with a laugh. "Of course, we know. Big fans."

"Thanks. I'm sorry you had to see that skating." She shuddered for a quick moment.

"Nonsense!" Tatiana exclaimed as she put her hands lightly on Jordan's shoulders. "Everybody has off days. You skated beautifully." Her voice was soft, comforting.

Jordan sighed, and turned away from her coach. "So you're new to the rink."

"Yes." Shelby perked up. "We're originally from Syracuse, but realized in order to get to the next level, we needed to move to a coach with more substance and experience."

"Well, Tatiana is the best. She's been with me almost my entire life. You couldn't be in better hands." There was a genuine affection between them. I shouldn't have been surprised. Tatiana was so concerned about Jordan that she contacted us. Then to my horror, Jordan focused on me. "So, Julian, how long have you been skating?"

It was then that I realized I hadn't said one word since we arrived.

I can do this. *My name is Julian Law. I am a figure skater.*

"Oh, yeah. Um, since I was little."

Scratch that: my name is John Watson and I need more

practice with this undercover stuff. Hey, at least I didn't tell her the truth: I haven't ice-skated yet, but if falling when rollerblading counted, I was a total pro.

"So!" Shelby pulled her chair closer to Jordan and leaned in like they were good friends. "We've never shared the ice with other skaters. Can you give us the scoop? I only know them from their skating reputations. Does everybody get along?"

Jordan nodded. "Yeah. I've known Douglas my whole life. We go to the rink together every morning and share the same tutor. He's been really supportive of my decision to go solo. He's a great guy. His new partner, Belle, is perfect for him. They're really great. I mean, I'm sure you guys are great."

Shelby laughed and I don't know how she did it, but she blushed. Could people blush on command?

Let me tell you, Shelby and I were great at many things, but skating wasn't going to be one.

"Doesn't Sergi have another skater?" Shelby prodded.

Jordan's mouth tightened. "Yes. Aisha."

Oh, who was this Aisha person? She seemed like bad news.

There was a knock on the door. Tatiana opened it to find Sergi Petrov. I recognized him from the photos Shelby showed me yesterday, although he was a little older. His white skin sported a few more wrinkles and his short black hair was gray around his temples. He wore a nylon Olympic jacket and paused when he saw us in the room.

"Oh, hello." He glanced at Shelby and me. "These your new skaters."

"*Da*," Tatiana replied. "This, um..." (Nice to know I wasn't the only one who had trouble with remembering aliases.)

Shelby stood up and held out her hand. "Roberta Downey and Julian Law, Mr. Petrov. Pleasure to meet you."

He took a step back and looked us both up and down. I sat up a bit straighter, wondering if he could figure out I wasn't a real skater by how I sat. I mean it's not that far-fetched—look what Shelby could do!

Sergi nodded. "Yes. You were impressive at the Carrier Dome Classic."

WE WERE WHAT?

"Thank you. It was one of our best performances," Shelby replied, while I tried to pick my jaw up from the floor.

The Carrier Dome what? Okay, I knew the Carrier Dome was in Syracuse. That's where our aliases were from. So . . . Oh wow. *Wow.* Sergi researched us on the internet. Just like Shelby suspected.

"Well, yes." He cleared his throat as he looked at Tatiana. He placed a brown paper bag on her desk. "Is medovik. I had extra and thought . . ."

Tatiana picked up the bag with two fingers as if it was dangerous. "No sugar. You know this."

Shelby perked up. "I'd love to try Russian honey cake."

Jordan's eyes got wide. "You eat desserts?"

"Only every once in a while as a treat," Shelby replied.

WHAT WAS GOING ON? There hasn't been a dessert that Shelby has ever turned down. EVER.

Sergi took back the bag and gave us a nod before leaving.

Hmm. So Sergi already did research on us and was still bringing his ex-wife treats. Although he knew she didn't eat sugar, so maybe he was trying to sabotage her. Either way, it was pretty suspicious behavior if you asked me.

"What wonderful team spirit," Shelby remarked after Sergi left. I knew what she was doing: she was hoping someone was going to say something bad about him.

"Listen," Jordan stated. *Here we go!* "We all respect each other and stay out of people's way when they're rehearsing. It'll probably take us a while to get into a good rhythm, but I look forward to sharing the ice with you on Monday."

Yeah, I don't think she'd be looking forward to it if she knew that we haven't even ice-skated yet.

"That's so nice of you," Shelby replied with a bat of her eyelashes. "I got worried about working with new skaters. I assumed there'd be trash-talking and unsportsmanlike conduct."

Jordan bristled. "Well, as a serious athlete you can't let that kind of stuff get to you." She abruptly stood up. "I need to get back to the ice. Nice to meet you."

She walked out, with Tatiana following quickly behind her.

"What do you think?" I asked once the door closed.

Shelby leaned back in her seat. "Jordan is definitely hiding something. And all those *greats*: oh, she's so *great*, he's a *great* guy . . ." Shelby stuck out her tongue. "Please. Nobody likes people that much."

"Um, Shelby, most people actually do like other people. I'd probably say that about my friends. They *are* great."

Shelby rolled her eyes. "Well, one of those *great* people sent her the cipher. And then there's Aisha. The only one she didn't use her favorite lackluster superlative to describe. Did you notice her demeanor when I mentioned trash-talking?"

"Yeah." It was kind of hard to miss: her shoulders tensed and she walked out not much later.

Shelby looked thoughtful. "While I still don't know what that message said, I can tell you one thing: it wasn't anything good."

CHAPTER 8

OUCH.

I put more ice on my hip. Ouch. Ouch. OUCH.

Shelby and I had decided to hit the skating rink this morning and yeah, it didn't go well. Um, okay, to be honest, it was a fiasco. I spent more time falling on my butt than skating. Shelby wasn't much better. After a couple hours, we were able to somewhat remain on our feet, as long as we didn't have to make any turns. Or skate backward. Or away from the safety of the sides.

In fairness to us, how was anybody supposed to be able to balance on a thin blade while gliding over ice? And, to make it even harder, the blade had these tiny claws at the front, which were used for jumps and footwork, but also made me fall. A lot. Every time it happened, Shelby would shout, "toe pick!" at me. Every. Single. Time.

This whole case might end up being one big disaster. And a pain. Especially for my hip.

And yeah, maybe my self-esteem.

To give my body a break, I'd been watching videos of Jordan skating. She was amazing. Her programs at nationals last year were pretty perfect—at least it seemed that way to me. Thinking about those big falls yesterday made me more determined to help her. I even watched some old footage of her and Douglas. Every time they'd finished a routine, they'd hold hands until they got to the area where they waited for the judges' scores (which I found out is called "kiss and cry" since those were two of the most likely things to happen after a skating performance). Jordan and Douglas would have their arms around each other, with Sergi and Tatiana flanking them. Once they got their scores, they'd do this playful shoulder bump and hand slap.

As much as a former partner would seem like our top suspect, they really appeared to get along. Jordan still hung out with Douglas all the time. It probably wasn't him.

But Jordan had left him . . .

My phone beeped. It was a message from Shelby. **I need you to come upstairs.**

Can't. Mom told me to wait for delivery, I replied.

While I didn't like having to sit in the apartment for whatever to be delivered, I was grateful this gave me some much needed time on the couch and off the skates.

The sound of stomping feet on the stairs meant that Shelby was coming to me.

I slowly sat up from the couch. I limped to the door, but then tried to set my face back to a normal position so Shelby couldn't tell how much pain I was in. While I wasn't thrilled that I had to pretend to be a figure skater, at least I was finally going undercover. I also felt bad for Jordan. She seemed nice, and it was clear that cipher was messing with her. I was itching to find out what it meant. And how we were going to crack it.

I opened the door and Shelby burst right in past me. I spun around to see what she was holding, but sucked in a breath as my hip throbbed. I realized I hadn't shut the door, but that was going to be too much effort so it was going to have to stay open.

"I need for you to—" She stopped and looked me up and down.

Here we go . . .

"I'm sure your mother can give you some acetaminophen to aid in your discomfort."

Gee, thanks for your concern, Shelby. And how was she not limping? She fell a few times, too. And it was as enjoyable to watch as you can imagine.

"Now back to business. I need you to try this on." She held up a red . . . something.

There were no words for this thing, as it was shiny and made of spandex. And sequins.

Wait. There were two words to describe this monstrosity and my thoughts about it. "No. Way," I replied with my arms folded. I meant it: there was *no way* she was getting me to wear that thing.

"Now, Watson, I spent considerable time sewing it. The least you could do—"

"The least I could do!" I snapped at her. "Shelby, I didn't hang out last night with my friends, so I could study figure

skaters and terms. I spent all this morning falling down. I am doing plenty. But I'm drawing the line at wearing something like that. People can skate in sweats."

"When you're undercover you must *become* your character, head to toe, including what you wear," she lectured.

I seriously think she enjoyed torturing me. Shelby knew everything, so she had to have anticipated I was not going to handle this well.

She stuck her hand on her hip. "Do you think I enjoy having to wear skirts and dresses and *smile* when I go undercover?"

Yeah, like those were the same things.

"Was this part of your plan? Are you doing all of this so I stop asking to go undercover?" My entire body hurt. I was sore and annoyed.

"Ah, Watson." Shelby stopped grimacing at me and pulled her shoulders back, like she realized something. Maybe I was getting through to her.

I wasn't going to lose my nerve. "I'm doing the best I can. So you're going to have to appreciate the effort I'm putting in and realize that there is no way on earth—*NO WAY*—that I can become a professional skater in a weekend, but more importantly that I will not be wearing that thing."

"Watson, turn around."

Oh, I wasn't going to fall for her tricks. "Why? So you can measure me?"

Shelby sighed. "Has he always been this dramatic?"

Wait. What did *that* even mean? I wasn't being dramatic. I was being rational.

Then I realized that Shelby wasn't even looking at me. Her gaze was over my shoulder and much higher than my eye line.

I slowly turned around.

I couldn't believe it. Maybe I was imagining things. I did hit my head pretty hard during one fall.

But, no. It was real. *He* was real.

"Hey, son."

⌁·CHAPTER·⌁
9

"Dad?"

Before I could really register what was happening, my dad gave me a hug.

My *dad*. Who was here.

"You've gotten so tall," he exclaimed, while I did everything Shelby had taught me about observing each detail about an event. I didn't want to forget this moment. "Surprised?" he asked with a laugh.

Surprised was an understatement.

"What? How?"

"I've been planning this for a couple weeks. I was supposed to come in yesterday, but my flight got canceled. Don't worry, you've got your old man for the whole week."

A whole week *with my dad*?

"Now don't tell me you forgot how to properly greet your pops?" He held his hand up, and it was like no time had passed. I slapped his hand high, then low. Tapped our right elbows together twice and then our lefts before we finished with a chest bump. It was our special greeting.

"That's my boy." Dad grabbed me around the neck and playfully rubbed my head. "Okay, now let me get a good look at you." He held me at a distance, his face full of pride. "My, my, my . . . You're soon going to be taller than me." I doubted that. Dad was really tall, over six feet. I had a ways to go.

He then turned his attention to Shelby. "And you must be the great Shelby Holmes."

"In the flesh," Shelby said as she gave my dad a nod. She then began to study him. I, in turn, gave her a look that made it clear my dad was off limits to her deductive reasoning. He just got here. I didn't want him running for the next flight home after Shelby was done with him.

Instead Shelby Holmes actually acted like a normal human being. For once. "Pleasure to meet you."

Dad wagged his finger at Shelby. "Listen here, you and I need to have a talk."

And there it was.

I knew Dad wasn't going to let what happened a couple weeks ago drop. I mean, it wasn't Shelby's fault that after a long day with very little food and water we got locked in a hot basement and I passed out from diabetic hypoglycemia. Okay, maybe some of it was Shelby's fault, but she got us out of there.

"Rightfully so," Shelby acknowledged.

While Shelby usually hated talking to, well . . . anybody about anything, she and Mom had a really nice conversation about me after the accident. Guess it was Dad's turn now.

"Well," Shelby said as she picked up that red excuse for a costume. "I know you two must have a lot of catching up to do, so I'll leave you to it. Tomorrow at four, Watson."

"You got it, Shelby."

She paused before leaving. "Have fun at the basketball game tonight." Then she shut the door behind her.

Dad's eyes were wide. "How did she know?"

"Know what?"

Dad pulled two tickets out of his jacket. "We're going to see the Knicks tonight."

I took the tickets. "Oh, cool!" I couldn't believe it. I was going to Madison Square Garden to watch a professional basketball game.

"How did she—"

"It's just this thing she does." I repeated a line I said to pretty much anybody when they first meet Shelby.

Dad looked around the apartment. I noticed he didn't have any luggage with him.

"You're not staying here?" I asked, disappointed.

"Nah, I'm at a hotel a few blocks away. I thought it would be better." He walked toward the back of the apartment where the bedrooms were. "I didn't think your mother had to work on the weekends anymore."

I shrugged. "She usually doesn't, but . . . Oh."

Dad flinched ever so slightly. It was something I would've missed two months ago, but now Shelby had trained me to notice the slightest facial tick.

But I also noticed something else. Mom could've been anywhere. "How did you know Mom was at work?"

"My little man." Dad held his arms out. "I'm your delivery."

So Mom knew Dad was coming and chose to work. She was avoiding him. Maybe I should've told Dad that Mom sometimes worked on the weekends. Or told him she did it to make sure he and I would have plenty of alone time together.

I could tell him all of that stuff, but neither of us would believe it.

Dad clapped his hands together. "Okay, my New York City man, what are we going to do?"

My mind raced with possibilities. I had dreamed of Dad coming to visit and showing him around. I couldn't believe he was really here.

"What do you want to see?"

He rubbed his bald head. "Everything."

I'd lived in four different states before Mom and I moved to New York. Harlem had been my home for only two months, but as I showed Dad around the neighborhood, I realized how much I'd already settled in.

"Thanks again, Sal!" I waved to the owner of a pizzeria as Dad and I left.

"Anytime, Watson!" he called after me.

"My little man knows all the important people," Dad said as he patted his belly. "It's true what they say, New York City has the best pizza in the world. I'm stuffed. Not like we won't have some hot dogs and popcorn at the game."

My face hurt from smiling so much, but I was really happy he was here. I know I looked like a fool grinning from ear to ear, but I didn't care.

"So," Dad said as he threw his arm over my shoulder. "How are you doing, John? Really?"

I had to think for a moment. I had friends. I had Shelby. I had Mom. My life here was actually great, but could I tell him that? Things would be better if he was here, but that wasn't going to happen. How would he feel if he knew I was getting by okay without him?

"It's all right, I guess."

"You can be happy, John." He nudged me. "You've already made all these friends, ones who give you and your pops free pizza." (I might've forgotten to tell him it was because of Shelby that Sal gave us free slices, or was why half the people who passed us waved at me.)

"I'm doing good."

"And your mom?" His eyes glanced down, indicating that he was uncomfortable. Apparently observing micro-facial expressions wasn't only helpful when talking to a suspect. It also worked with your parents.

"Yeah. She's good, too."

Should I tell him how much I missed him? He and I didn't get mushy like that. We played ball. We watched sports. We didn't have these big heart-to-heart talks.

We kept walking as I struggled to come up with something to say. We never had this problem before. Usually I'd tell him about school or he'd tell me what happened at the recruiting office. He always had funny stories about the interviews he'd have with people interested in joining the army. A lot thought that the second they'd enlisted they'd be given these huge guns and go off to beat the bad guys. One dude even said to Dad, "You expect me to go to training?" Dad's go-to reply would always be, "You expect to ever get a job someday?"

"How's work?" I asked to cut through the quiet.

"It's work," Dad replied with a shake of his head.

Then silence.

Followed by even more uncomfortable silence.

"So!" Dad said as we were stopped at a crosswalk. "What are you and Shelby up to? I'm assuming that argument you were in earlier was about a case?"

"Yeah!" The case! I could talk to my dad about our case. "We have a new one we're working on. We have to decrypt this cipher that an athlete got. Her coach, who was an Olympian, came to us after she read that article I sent you." I started standing a bit taller even talking about it. Sparkly costumes aside, it was a pretty cool case. Even if it was causing me to fall on my butt. A lot.

"Olympic athletes! What sport?"

Great.

I continued to babble so I didn't have to answer that question. "And we're even going undercover. Which I've been waiting to do."

"Look at you. You planning on joining the CIA when you're out of college? FBI?"

I laughed. I'd never really thought about it. Maybe I did have a future as an actual, real-life spy. I bet covert CIA operatives never have to wear sequins.

"What sport is it? Because I know Shelby is some sort of genius, but no way can she compete with my boy on the field or court."

I continued to laugh even harder. It was mostly forced, but it was also because Dad was right. I could beat Shelby at any sport, except maybe figure skating.

"Well, it's not really a sport on a court or field." He was going to find out eventually. "It's on the ice."

"Hockey!" Dad guessed. "Can't say I know much about hockey, but you better make sure you wear plenty of padding. Those hockey players play rough."

I took a deep breath. "It's not hockey. It's . . . figure skating."

Dad stopped walking. "Hold up, hold up. Are you telling me that my son is going undercover as a figure skater?"

I couldn't say it aloud. So I nodded my head ever so slightly.

Dad's face was frozen for a few seconds. He may have not even taken a single breath.

"Dad . . . ?"

Finally, a huge grin broke onto his face. "This, I've *got* to see!"

CHAPTER 10

THE IMPOSSIBLE HAPPENED: A COMPROMISE HAD BEEN reached.

I could wear sweats while we were undercover, but they couldn't, as Shelby dictated, "have the grotesque logo of any professional or intramural sporting organization."

Hey, that was something I could agree to. Anything that kept me out of spandex.

But that meant we needed to go back to the ice to practice before we had to skate in front of actual figure skaters tomorrow morning.

"Good afternoon," Shelby greeted Dad and me with a slight lift of her chin.

"Oh, hey, Shelby," I said as I pulled her away so we could talk in private. "Do you mind if my dad comes along? He wouldn't get in the way. He just wants to see us work."

Shelby looked over at my dad, who was busy typing on his phone. "From what I've been able to gather about talented child athletes, there's usually a parent hovering around them, so his audience wouldn't be questioned. We'd just have to fill him in on his alibi."

This was getting better and better. My first undercover assignment and I got to do it with my dad!

"Ready to go?" Shelby marched past us, not waiting for a reply.

"You know, Shelby," Dad said as he caught up to her. Shelby walked fast, so Dad practically had to jog to reach her. "I'd love to meet your parents while I'm here. Maybe after this, you could introduce me?"

"Believe me, Mr. Watson, once you cross paths with my parents, they will force an invitation on you for dinner. They love to have people over."

"Sounds like your parents are fun."

"That could be one word to describe them. I have others." Shelby's nose scrunched up. Mom and I had been to the Holmeses' a few times for dinner. Mr. and Mrs. Holmes liked to entertain, while Shelby preferred to be locked in a room reading or studying. Most people were a nuisance to her. Her brother, Michael, felt the same way about guests. So yeah, they were a barrel of joy during our dinners.

"What about—" Dad stopped talking as we rounded the corner to Adam Clayton Powell Jr. Boulevard as Mom was coming up the street. They hadn't seen each other since he arrived yesterday. They somehow kept missing one another. Mom made it seem like an accident, but I could tell she didn't want to see him.

It took Mom a few more moments to realize we were approaching. I could hardly breathe as I waited for her to see Dad. They'd spoken on the phone a few times, but it was always about me. And when we first moved here, it was mostly Mom yelling at Dad for not calling when he said he would.

Mom finally looked up and froze. A look of sadness flashed on her face before she forced a smile, which I knew was only for my benefit.

"Hello, John and Shelby . . . Martin." She gave a little nod.

"Hey, Janice," Dad replied. He could hardly look at her.

This was awful.

And really, *really* uncomfortable.

Shelby looked over at me, and I don't know what I did or what she saw in my face, but whatever it was, I was grateful for it.

"We really have to move along," Shelby said as she tapped her watch. "Dr. Watson, I'm afraid that we're running late for a very important appointment. No dillydallying, gentlemen."

Shelby took Dad by the elbow. "Did Watson ever tell

you about the time I found the culprit who had robbed Sal's? It was one of my finest moments."

Shelby dragged Dad down the block, while he kept looking back at Mom.

"Have fun," Mom said to me. She bent down to kiss my forehead. "Good luck skating. And stay safe."

She walked back toward our apartment without so much as a glance over her shoulder at Dad.

So that was that.

My parents couldn't even be on the same sidewalk. It stung to know that there was no way they'd ever get back together.

I know, I know. We lived in different states. They've been separated for almost a year, but now that Dad was here, I could fool myself into thinking that things were back to normal. I had my time with him. I had my time with Mom.

But I was never going to have my time together with them both again. Just the three of us. Like a family.

CHAPTER
11

IT WAS TIME.

Granted, I wished that time wasn't five o'clock in the morning. Nobody should be up that early. Nobody.

I had a piece of peanut butter toast in my mouth and an apple in my jacket pocket as I met Shelby outside our apartment building. The sky was dark, like it was midnight.

As much as it hurt to realize my parents were incapable of being around each other, I had to concentrate on the case.

It was one of the few things I could control.

"Are you seriously eating candy right now?" I asked Shelby, who had chocolate smeared on her chin.

"Breakfast of champions," she replied. "Is your dad coming?"

"Not when he found out what time." Because my dad was sane. And asleep. I was going to see him after school when the sun was out.

As we turned on Lenox to head to the subway, I was

surprised by the cars on the street. I guess it was true: New York was a city that never slept.

Oh, how I wanted to go back to sleep.

I wasn't the only one. Unlike during our visit on Friday, the Sky Rink was currently deserted.

Because why on earth would anything be open this early in the morning?

Even though the reception area was dark, as we headed toward the rink I wished I had brought sunglasses. It was bright. The overhead fluorescent lights lit up the white ice.

It was the first time I was able to properly see Shelby. Besides having her hair tamed up in a bun like during our meeting with Jordan, she had something on her face that made her skin sparkle.

"Glitter," Shelby replied as she stuck her tongue out in disgust. "Sometimes playing a part can be quite a humiliating affair."

This from the girl who wanted me to wear red sequins?

"Okay, Julian," Shelby said in her sweet Roberta voice. "I'll meet you on the ice." She gestured to the boys' locker room.

Now a locker room was somewhere I felt comfortable. I walked in and found a locker to store my book bag (since we had to go to school after) and shoes. I put my skates on and felt pretty good that I stayed on my feet.

The door to the locker room opened and a tall white guy a few years older than me with blond hair and blue eyes walked in. It was Douglas. He had on black spandex leggings. (This "sport." I mean, really?)

"Hello." He extended his hand. "You must be part of the new pairs team working with Tatiana."

"Yes, I'm Jo—Julian. Julian Law." Phew. That was close. I couldn't believe I almost blew my cover after two minutes.

"I'm Douglas. My partner and I work with Sergi."

"Yeah. Nice to meet you."

Okay, I had to admit, I was just a tad awestruck. This dude, despite his current outfit, was strong. The lifts he did and his jumps were kind of unbelievable.

I followed Douglas out to the two rinks.

"Have a good skate," Douglas said before he went out on the rink to the left.

But to say that he was skating was an understatement. Douglas was practically flying across the ice. He was skating backward, in circles, and then jumped and landed like he was floating. Sergi was skating near him and barking commands. Then, a tiny white girl with black hair up in a fancy bun joined him. He picked her up and held her over his head like she weighed nothing.

We were in so much trouble. No way anybody would believe Shelby and I were pairs skaters. No way.

I looked over to my right and it took me a second to recognize Shelby. She had on white tights with a purple skirt and wrapped sweater. She looked like a ballerina.

I clobbered over to her in my skates. "I think we should pretend one of us is injured," I reasoned with her. "I'll volunteer to sit out."

Shelby ignored my suggestion. (Hey, it was worth a shot.)

I looked over to where Jordan and Tatiana were in a huddle on the ice. Then I glanced back at Sergi's rink.

It was all so . . . white.

But before I could say anything to Shelby, another skater entered Sergi's rink. She had big brown eyes and her hair was in twists that were gathered in a giant bun on top of her head. She looked to be around my age. She skated with such speed and grace. With a dimpled smile on her face, she looked like she loved every moment on the ice. I couldn't keep my eyes off her. She then started twirling in a circle so fast, I almost got dizzy watching her.

"You might want to wipe the drool off your face," Shelby said as she pretended to gag. "Try to focus, Julian."

Whatever. I was only studying her. Wasn't that what I was supposed to do? I wasn't drooling. I mean, the skater was pretty impressive. Strong. Confident. Okay, okay, and like, yeah, maybe she was pretty or, you know, whatever.

"Excuse me!" a voice called out from behind us.

Shelby and I turned around to see a white woman with fuzzy lavender earmuffs holding up a giant video recorder. (Hadn't she heard of a camera phone?) "Who are you and what are you doing here? This is a closed practice."

She did not look happy to see us. Although who could really be happy at this hour?

"What are your names? Who are you spying for?" she continued her interrogation, although she wasn't giving us a chance to answer.

Which was good because I was about to panic. This woman already knew we were up to something. Shelby, as always, kept her cool.

"I'm Roberta Downey and this is my partner, Julian Law. We're new to Tatiana and just moved from outside Syracuse. We were simply admiring your daughter—"

"Sergi!" the older woman called out over Shelby. "I don't want this competition watching Belle and Douglas skate."

Hmm . . . this woman was wigging out. Why? Possible suspect?

"Mrs. Booth." Tatiana approached us, as did every other skater in the rink. "These new skaters. I told you they come. They skate, but not like Belle and Douglas. No competition."

("No competition" was probably the biggest understatement of the millennium.)

"Mom, let them skate," the tiny girl who was skating

with Douglas, who I deduced was Belle, said in a soft voice. I should've known they were mother and daughter. They were practically dressed as twins. Both were wearing lavender head to toe. Belle was in a skating outfit with sequins (seriously, what was with this sport and sequins?). Her mom had a puffy lavender jacket with matching leggings. Her hair was up in the same fancy bun.

"I've never heard of these people," said Mrs. Booth.

Jordan, who had been skating near the side, finally stopped. "Mrs. Booth, I met with them on Friday. They're a very sweet pair."

"Oh well, if *you* know them, Jordan," Mrs. Booth replied with a little flutter, like she was starstruck.

"Moooom," Belle groaned, clearly embarrassed by what was happening.

"Do not give them a second look, darling." Mrs. Booth held up her recorder. "Back to skating. We have a competition to win on Saturday."

"Mom—" Belle tried to get a word in, but her mom continued to talk over her.

"Skate, not talk." Mrs. Booth pointed toward the ice. "You can talk after you get first place."

Belle narrowed her green eyes at her mom before she skated off. Sergi studied us for a few moments before he turned back to Douglas and Belle.

The other girl was still staring at us.

"Oh, um, hi—" I cleared my throat. "Yeah, I'm—"

"Julian," the girl said with a laugh. "And you're Roberta. I'm Aisha. Nice to meet you." She stole a glance at Belle's mom before whispering, "You'll get used to Mrs. Booth. She can be a bit . . . intense."

"Duly noted," Shelby replied with a nod.

"Yeah, ah . . ."

What was wrong with me? Why couldn't I speak? I've talked to a ton of girls before. I mean not a ton or anything, but this was getting embarrassing.

Besides, this was Aisha, who Jordan didn't have anything "great" to say about.

"See you around," Aisha replied with a small wave as she went back to center ice.

"Very smooth, Julian," Shelby snorted.

I glared at Shelby. She wasn't making any of this easier on me. And it wasn't like I was doing something weird or anything.

Whatever.

"Something's wrong," Shelby stated as she motioned with her jaw to Jordan. Jordan was speeding up again, but before she even took off for a jump, she stopped. Tatiana skated next to her and put her arm around her. The two of them skated slowly around the rink, arm and arm.

"This is good, Watson," Shelby remarked. "This means she got another message."

It didn't look like it was good for Jordan.

Tatiana skated over to us while Jordan spun in the middle of the rink.

"Roberta and Julian," Tatiana said slowly to ensure she got our aliases right this time. "Today, no skating. Orientation of rink."

Thank you!

"Jordan," Tatiana called out, "Practice components of short program. I show them around."

Shelby and I followed Tatiana toward the coach's office. Once we were out of earshot, Shelby said, "When did she get the new message?"

Tatiana paused before unlocking the door. "How you know this?"

"It seemed rather obvious with her skating."

Tatiana's shoulders sagged. "She upset all morning. Distracted. I went in bag and found this."

She handed us a crumpled piece of paper with another cipher on it:

Shelby pulled the old cipher out of the boot of her skate and began to compare the two. Her eyes darted back and forth. "This might help us crack it."

"Really?" I asked.

"Do you see that in the new one, there's one character by itself." Shelby pointed at the lone figure. "So we may know what *A* or *I* is."

"It could be a number," I added.

Shelby grimaced. "Yes, it could. Regardless, I'll work on it at lunch. I wish we had more ciphers to work with."

"No more," Tatiana said with a wave of her hands. "Jordan too upset."

"But don't you want to know what this person is saying to her?"

"Yes, but my Jordan. I want it to stop. I want her back to herself."

"The only way that can happen is by cracking this cipher. Correct me if I'm wrong, but isn't that why you came to us?"

Tatiana nodded. "Yes. But, ticktock. We have no time. Regionals in five days. Five."

I wasn't sure how we were going to be able to figure this cipher out in five days. Or ever.

Although I knew to never underestimate Shelby. She'd find a way.

But it wasn't going to be enough to decode it. We had to find out who was leaving it. It was clear the ciphers were pretty short. Only a few words. I doubted the person was signing them.

I kept thinking about Belle's mom being so overprotective. "Tatiana, why was Mrs. Booth upset we're here?"

"She very insecure," Tatiana replied. "Belle is Douglas's third partner since Jordan."

Three partners in less than a year? That seemed like a lot.

"Who is Jordan's prime competition?" I asked.

"Aisha," Tatiana replied. "They always first and second. Jordan is first sometimes, sometimes Aisha."

Shelby raised her eyebrow at me.

But, hold on, maybe that's why Jordan didn't like Aisha, because they're rivals. Aisha seemed all right to me.

"I need to go to Jordan," Tatiana said. "But take your time. And lock up."

Shelby nodded as she studied the ciphers some more.

Okay, so let me make sure I had this straight: Jordan used to skate with Douglas, who now had a partner with a jealous mom. Sergi used to coach Jordan, but now Jordan was coached by Sergi's ex-wife. Aisha, who was Jordan's main competition, was also coached by Sergi.

Yikes. This was a pretty crazy web of people.

"Shelby," I asked although I felt I already knew what the answer would be, "who's our main suspect?"

Shelby looked up from the ciphers and smirked. "All of them."

Yep, that's what I thought.

⌐·CHAPTER·⌐
12

I WAS EXHAUSTED. I WAS ALSO TOTALLY TURNED AROUND.

The Empire State Building had always been downtown from me in Harlem. But now it was uptown.

As much as it took a few minutes to get my bearings, I had to admit: this view was amazing. Yeah, I still was in awe of Manhattan, but I think what made it even better was the person I was with.

"Sure is something, huh?" Dad said as he took in the skyline.

He met up with me after school and took me downtown to these really cool elevated train tracks that ran along the west side of the city. I guess they used to be abandoned, but were turned into a park a few years ago. Shelby put it on a list of places for Dad to take me. Of course, he didn't ask her for a list, but we were both happy to have it.

Tomorrow we were going to walk across the Brooklyn Bridge to get pizza. Shelby was very specific about which pizza place we should go to. I had thought pizza was pizza, but I wasn't about to question Shelby.

Even though I was functioning on little sleep, I wasn't too tired when I was with Dad. I was happy.

Walking around these old train tracks reminded me of when I was little. I was obsessed with cars and trucks, but especially trains. Dad used to take me to train tracks near our old post in Texas. I must've been five or six, and we'd sit there and count each trailer. One time there was this huge train that had exactly one hundred and sixty-four cars. Afterward, he drove us over a half hour out of our way to get me sugar-free ice cream.

It was one of my favorite moments with him.

Just like now.

"Let's sit over here," Dad said as he gestured toward these rows of elevated benches. It looked like seating for a play or something, but instead of a stage, we looked out of this giant glass window that showed the street below. A ton of taxis and cars whizzed underneath us.

"Remember how you used to love cars?" Dad asked.

"And trains," I added.

"Pretty much anything that moved." He put his arm around me. "It's so good hanging with my son."

I didn't know what to say. These last couple days meant everything to me, but . . .

Yeah, there was a *but*.

Mom.

Hanging out with Dad meant that I was with Mom less. She kept telling me she wanted me to spend this time with him, but that meant I left her behind. It wasn't fair to her. But it also wasn't fair to me. Why did I have to decide between them? *I* wasn't the one who wanted the dumb divorce.

I looked at Dad as he studied the traffic below.

Even with all the work I'd been doing for the case, I did find a few minutes today at school to do some other kind of research.

I decided to go for broke. "Did you know that there's an army post in New York City? Fort Hamilton. It's in Brooklyn and only a little over an hour subway ride to Harlem."

Dad's gaze stayed fixed on the road. He wouldn't look at me.

That was not a good sign.

After a few more moments of silence, he finally replied, "Is that right?"

I nodded, but he still wouldn't look at me.

"You're such a smart boy. When did you get to be smarter than your old man?"

Did that mean he never thought about moving here to be with us?

He finally turned to me. "My son, the decoder! That's some serious spy stuff you're doing."

Well, I wasn't really a decoder since we still didn't know what the cipher said. Although I was taking whatever compliments Dad had for me. Besides, I knew he was changing the subject. It was pretty obvious that was what he was doing.

I forced a smile since I didn't want him to know how much it upset me. "Yeah, it's pretty cool."

"When you showed me that first—what's it called again?"

"Cipher."

Dad smiled as he shook his head. "You sound like someone on TV. *Cipher. Decryption. Codes.*"

Yeah, it *was* cool. I decided to focus on the positive. This case was bigger than anything we had ever worked on. There were so many people who could be the culprit. We were working for an Olympic gold medalist (yeah, besides researching army posts, I also looked up Tatiana and Sergi—they were the real deal . . . when they were together). At least something in my life was moving forward.

As much as Tatiana didn't want any more ciphers, I did. I wanted to see if we could crack it. Shelby didn't get anywhere at lunch today. She didn't need to tell me that. It was clear when she stood up in the middle of lunch and ripped up a notebook. Shelby was good at many things, but hiding her annoyance wasn't one of them.

What did those notes say? And why was Jordan keeping it a secret from Tatiana?

And how did I keep coming up with more unanswered questions?

Dad started laughing. "I don't know much about figure skating. The only time I watched it was years ago. Back in the dark ages before I even met your mother."

Oh, right. Sometimes I forgot that my parents were once kids, too.

Dad leaned back on the bench. "It was right before the Olympics. This one skater was leaving practice and got attacked. Some thug hit her in the knee right before a competition."

"Whoa," I replied.

"Yeah, it ended up being this big deal. It was all over the news. Then it came out that the person who orchestrated the attack was the ex-husband of her main rival."

"Are you serious?"

Dad nodded. "Yeah. Then they both went to the Olympics."

"Wait," I interrupted him. "That other girl still got to compete? That's not fair!"

"No, it wasn't. Her name was Tonya Harding. She

claimed that she was innocent and didn't know, you know, blah, blah, blah. But it didn't matter. She didn't do well and in the end got kicked out of skating. That is what you call karma, my boy."

Okay, that was unreal.

"What about the lady who got injured?"

"Nancy Kerrigan," Dad said with a nod of respect. "She rallied and ended up getting a silver medal."

Wow. I tried to imagine getting injured and coming back to win something.

Okay, I'll admit that I totally thought figure skating wasn't a real sport. My mind started changing after putting on skates and watching the dedication of the skaters at the rink. But this was next level.

Figure skaters were tough.

Dad shook his head. "Let me tell you something, figure skaters look all prim and proper. But they are not to be messed with, especially when it comes to competition."

No kidding.

CHAPTER 13

I NEVER UNDERSTOOD WHY MOM LIKED COFFEE SO MUCH. IT smelled gross. It looked even worse, like sludge. Yuck.

But now I totally got it. I almost poured myself a huge cup before leaving for Chelsea Piers the next morning. Even after crashing at eight o'clock last night, I was dragging my feet as Shelby and I arrived at six.

Again, that was six o'clock. *In the morning.*

"Today, we need to find out as much as we can about everybody in that rink. Everybody, and I mean *everybody,* is a suspect until I say otherwise." Shelby paused outside the main door to the building. "Since we are four days away from regionals, this is what I see as our options at this point. One, we wait for the culprit to mess up. Two, we come early and hide to see if we can catch them in the act of leaving a cipher. Or three, come clean about who we are, to see the changes that happen. The guilty person would obviously act differently."

"I vote number three," I said quickly. I couldn't imagine getting up even earlier than we'd been. No way did I want to be waiting around a cold rink in hopes that we could catch the person. Knowing our luck, we'd miss it. Most likely because I would be in a deep sleep.

I really missed sleep.

"Number three is our last option. I always find it most beneficial when people are left in the dark," Shelby fired back. "If they think we're simply amateur skaters, they won't try to throw us off their scent. We want this miscreant to think no one is on to them."

Of course Shelby wanted to leave people in the dark. I could never follow her scent. And I was her partner!

"See you on the ice," Shelby stated as she walked into the girls' locker room.

After changing into my skates, I lumbered over to the rink. I'd gotten a little more comfortable in my skates. In a few weeks, I'd probably stop falling. But this case could NOT go on for that long. Regionals were on Saturday. We had to find the person. If Jordan continued to miss her jumps, her season would be done.

One spill and BAM. Game over.

Aisha was in the middle of skating to music while Jordan, Douglas, and Belle sat together on a bench watching something on a phone. They were all laughing. It was something

91

I'd do with my friends. Maybe they were this family like Jordan had told us.

Once the music stopped and Aisha's program or whatever she was skating to was finished, Sergi skated over to the entrance of the rink. "Enough break! You break after regionals."

Tatiana came in from the hallway. "You do not boss my skater around."

Sergi's eyes narrowed. "Well, your skater distract mine."

"We're going!" Belle was the first of the group to hit the ice.

Jordan and Douglas exchanged a look, like siblings who were embarrassed that their parents were fighting. Then they did that hand-thing I saw on the video. After, he put his arm around her shoulder as they approached the divide between their rinks. "You've got this."

"I hope," Jordan replied with a frown.

"You know." Douglas nudged her.

"Thanks. And you guys are looking great. Belle, your axel is tight."

Before Belle could reply, her mom piped up. "She doesn't get as much height as you, Jordan."

Sergi blew a whistle, a very loud whistle, and everybody got back to work. Tatiana pulled Jordan aside and whispered to her, stroking her hair. Jordan shook her head fiercely before getting back out onto the ice.

That couldn't be a good sign.

Aisha came off the ice to sit down and retied her skates.

"Hey," I said with a nod of my chin.

Real suave, Watson.

She looked up and gave me a smile. And, okay, I'll admit that she was cute and all, but she could be the enemy.

And, well, my record with befriending the culprit wasn't so great. I mean, it wasn't my fault my first non-Shelby friend here stole his sister's dog.

"We didn't get a chance to really talk yesterday." Aisha smiled at me. "I've never seen you guys around the circuit. But I guess I've always done singles, so I only know the pairs I share the ice with."

"Yeah, well . . . um, we're new to the city." Yeah, I was killing it being undercover. (NOT.)

"Where do you live now?" she asked as she batted her long eyelashes at me.

This wasn't good. I was supposed to be interrogating her, yet I wasn't really used to talking to such pretty girls. And she was a *girl*. Dressed head to toe in pink.

"Harlem," I answered.

"We're neighbors," Aisha said. "I'm in Morningside Heights. But my dad works in Harlem. Well, one of his two jobs."

That surprised me. I automatically assumed all these figure skaters were rich and lived on Park Avenue or Central Park West. Shelby had informed me that both Douglas and Jordan grew up in wealthy families. That made sense. This sport couldn't have been cheap: coaches, private ice time, skates, outfits, and choreography. And that was solely what I knew from the little research I'd done. I was lucky the sports I was into only required a ball. Which you could share.

I had that sinking feeling in my gut. Did Aisha have another motive to send Jordan messages? They were each other's biggest competition. Aisha didn't have the money Jordan did. She needed to win more.

Aisha stood up and shook her legs out. "I guess I better get back to work. See you around, Julian." She gave me a wink before skating out onto the ice. She was graceful. She was strong. She was extraordinary.

I was making things worse. Shelby had told me more than once to not get involved with clients or suspects. But I wasn't getting involved. I was doing my job.

Yep, that was all I was doing.

"Anything?" Shelby asked as she stretched near the entrance to where Jordan had been skating since we arrived.

I hesitated for a second before finally replying, "Maybe."

Shelby tilted her head. "Oh, this is precious. Julian Law, do you have a crush?" She then pretended to throw up.

I ignored her. "There might be a money issue with Aisha. Her dad works two jobs."

Shelby studied Aisha as she skated. "Money is a powerful motivator for any suspect. Well done!"

Weird. I didn't feel that great about discovering a motive.

Tatiana came over to us. "Roberta and Julian, there is something you need to see in the equipment room."

"I presumed there would be," Shelby replied with a confident smirk.

Shelby and I walked over to the room. As soon as we turned the light on, we saw a cipher on a whiteboard.

Shelby approached the cipher and studied it closely.

She folded her arms. "Well, it looks like the decision has been made for us."

I looked at the cipher, confused. "What decision?"

"We are going with number one, Watson. The perpetrator has made a mistake."

⌐ CHAPTER ·⌐
14

THERE IT WAS: A SMUDGE.

A mistake.

A clue.

You might be wondering how a smudge could be a big deal. I would've thought the same thing two months ago.

Now, I knew better.

Shelby's face was barely an inch away from the cipher. "This is the first time the person has used a whiteboard instead of pen on paper. Now we know that they're left-handed."

"How?" I asked.

Shelby flipped over the whiteboard and started writing with her right hand. "A right-handed person wouldn't have left a smudge. However, a left-handed culprit, especially in the case of a wet marker, would . . ." She started writing with her left hand. Her left palm came in contact with the board and made a similar smudge.

"You know what this also means?" She held up her stained hand.

"If the person wrote the cipher this morning, they'd now have blue ink stain on their left hand."

This was good. This was going to get us somewhere.

"There's more," Shelby stated as she flipped the whiteboard back to the cipher and pointed at the top four lines. "This was written by a different person than this one." She tapped at the bottom one.

"How can you tell?" I asked as I started to examine the drawings.

"There are slight differences. First, not a single smudge on the bottom line. Second, the characters are slightly bigger, as well as the lines for the hands are straight, not curved like above. Different handwriting, different person. So it appears that Jordan has answered back." Shelby was practically giddy.

"But what exactly did Jordan answer? And, you know, what was the question?"

Shelby took a photo of the board with her phone. "I think I finally have enough to figure it out."

"Really?"

"After school, Watson. We're going to crack this thing."

"We are!" Finally!

"Soon we'll know what is being communicated, but for now, we need to see if we can deduce who left it."

Yes, now to the business at hand of finding the culprit. And I do mean at *hand*.

"How are we going to be able to examine everybody's left hand without them knowing what we're up to? Especially since . . ." I wiggled my hands in my gloves. We all wore gloves on the ice because it was cold. "Maybe we should just come clean and demand to see everybody's hands?"

Shelby shook her head. "Absolutely not." She closed her eyes for a few minutes, something she did when she was trying to figure out a plan or access something in her brain attic. Shelby opened her eyes and clapped her hands together. "Okay, this is what we're going to do. We are obviously big fans of these skaters."

"We are?" That was news to me.

Shelby scowled. "Well, Roberta and Julian certainly would be."

Oh, right. Yes.

Shelby continued, "So when they take a break, you are going to ask each one of them for an autograph and a picture."

"Why do I—"

Shelby kept talking over me. "However, I'll be recording a video instead of a photograph. We will ask them some basic question as they're signing their autograph and posing. It is difficult for people to keep lies straight when they are doing two things at once. One of the best tactics when interrogating someone is to have them do another task to distract them. We can analyze the video for micro-facial expressions when we are finished."

It sounded like a pretty solid plan, but . . .

"Can't you ask for the autographs?" I asked. I mean, I didn't know how well I could pretend I was this gigantic fan. I'd never been the kind of guy to gush. Not like Shelby ever dared compliment someone else, but she was better at this acting stuff than me.

Shelby waved her hand away. "Just pretend that they're one of the basketball performers you admire."

"But—"

"Watson," Shelby stated, and it was clear her patience was wearing thin. "It has to be you."

"Why?"

"Isn't it obvious?"

Um, no. Unless it was because Shelby loved nothing more than making me look foolish. Because *that* was obvious.

"You're going to make me say it, aren't you?"

Ah, yeah, because I had no idea what she was getting at.

Shelby sighed. "You need to be the one to do it, because you are much better with people than I am."

Oh, yeah.

Well, she had me there.

CHAPTER 15

SO THIS WAS EMBARRASSING.

I waited until Douglas took a break to approach him. I'd had no clue who this dude was only a few days ago, but now I had to pretend to be this huge fan. There was no way he was going to fall for it.

"Hey, man."

"Hey," Douglas replied, but his focus was on Jordan, who was gliding across the ice, moving her arms all gracefully. She took a giant leap, twirled once in the air, and came back down on her foot, wobbling a bit before getting her balance. "You got this!" Douglas shouted at Jordan with a fist pump. He then lowered his voice. "Now she just needs to get back to nailing her triple jumps."

"Focus on this rink!" Sergi said as he pointed to Belle, who was doing some twirly thing.

Douglas clenched his jaw as he turned his attention toward his partner.

I guess this was my chance. "Yeah, so this may sound silly"—*because it was*—"but I'm a huge fan and I was wondering if I could get your picture . . . and an autograph."

Douglas paused from taking a sip of water. He blinked a few times before giving me a nod. "Of course."

Or maybe he had an ego like most athletes and assumed everybody was an admirer.

Shelby hovered nearby with her phone, so there would be proof of me making a fool out of myself.

Awesome.

"Let me just take this off." Douglas removed his blue headband and then smoothed out his hair.

"Here's your autograph book," Shelby said as she handed me this pink sparkly notebook.

Come on! Pink? Sparkly? Shelby was going to be in so much trouble for that.

"Yeah, ah," I stuttered as I handed Douglas the notebook and a black pen.

Douglas took off his gloves and I tried to examine his left hand, but he picked up the pen with his right.

It wasn't him.

Or maybe he wrote the cipher with his left hand? Or maybe he accidentally brushed up against the board?

Shelby cleared her throat, which meant I wasn't doing what I was supposed to do: ask him questions while he was distracted. First, I had to start with easy stuff. We had to know what his normal expressions were before we started talking about Jordan in case there was a change.

"So I used to skate after school," I stated. "How long did it take you to get used to these early mornings?"

"A couple weeks."

A couple weeks? We didn't have that much time. And there was no way I wanted my alarm clock blasting at five a.m. to be normal for me.

"I believe it's important to be first on the ice." Douglas's eyes stayed focused on the autograph book. "I can sleep after the Olympics."

So, he was here first thing in the morning and could've left the cipher before anybody else got here.

"Yeah." I laughed. "Your dedication is insane."

"Thank you," he replied coolly as he wrote *best wishes* to Julian.

Huh. Douglas seemed really warm and friendly around Jordan and Belle, but he was not to me. What was he hiding? Or maybe he was being distant toward me because he thought I was competition? Because, like, as soon as he saw me "skate," he'd realize what a joke that was.

Guess it was time to bring up Jordan.

"Was it hard switching partners?" I asked.

Douglas glanced at Shelby, probably wondering if I was

thinking of leaving her (the thought had recently crossed my mind—see: sparkly pink notebook).

But then it happened.

It was like a double whammy of micro-facial expressions. Douglas paused, looked to the right (which meant he was lying!), and then said, "It was for the best" while shaking his head slightly (a signal that he didn't believe what he was saying!).

BINGO!

He didn't want to skate with Belle. He wanted to skate with Jordan. And if she didn't do well this weekend, she might go back to skating pairs with him! Maybe he had someone else write the cipher, or he could've written with his left hand to hide his handwriting!

Douglas handed me my notebook and put his arm around me as we posed for a picture.

"Thank you," Shelby said as she approached Douglas. She grabbed his hands in hers. "You have no idea how much Julian admires you. He's very shy when he meets his heroes. He burst into tears after meeting David Pelletier."

I nodded like I had any idea who Shelby was talking about.

Shelby kept holding his hands, but Douglas took a step back. She turned his hands over and put them to her chin. "Thank you for being such an inspiration."

Yeah, she was laying it on pretty thick, but she was getting a good look at his hands, which were as clean as could be.

Shelby dropped his hands and approached Aisha, who was over to the side stretching. Huh. Aisha never seemed to hang out with any of the other skaters. When they took breaks, Douglas, Belle, and Jordan would talk or show each other things on their phones, but Aisha was always by herself.

Ugh, yet another mark in the column against her.

"Aisha, Julian is a huge fan. Would you—"

Sergi came skating over, glaring at Shelby and me. What did this guy have against us? He would have the most motivation of messing with Jordan. If Jordan failed, one of his skaters would have a better chance of winning, he might even get Jordan back, and it would be revenge against his ex.

Maybe it was Sergi!

"Aisha, you do program again now!" he barked.

"Sorry," Aisha said to us before hitting the rink.

As Belle came off the ice, Shelby approached her. "Belle, Julian is a huge fan. Would you be willing to sign his autograph book?"

Douglas grimaced. I didn't blame him. I was apparently a *huge* fan of everybody. Except, at that moment, Shelby.

"Of course," Belle said with a warm smile. "I'm always happy to take time with my fans."

Jordan passed by us on the rink as she did this crazy stuff with her feet. Douglas's eyes were glued to her. He really seemed to focus on Jordan. Although I had to admit, she was pretty impressive . . . when she stayed on her feet.

"Are you also going to have Jordan sign your book?" Belle asked. But before I could even reply, she added, "Because it would be best to keep her on your good side."

"Belle," Douglas cautioned. "We don't have proof."

Shelby raised her eyebrows. "Proof of what?"

Belle leaned in. "Just don't leave your skates alone around her. Aisha made the mistake of using the bathroom before her short program at nationals, and then her shoelace broke right before she took to the ice."

"Shoelaces break," Douglas reasoned.

"But they were new," Belle replied with a smirk.

I couldn't look at Shelby. If what Belle said was true, Aisha now had the biggest motive to throw Jordan off her game.

"Do you want me to sign this to Julian?" Belle asked as she took the notebook from me.

"Belle." Mrs. Booth came over, a stern look on her face. "After the disastrous run-through of twenty minutes ago, you need to be practicing your axel, not goofing around. Look at Jordan, she's focused."

Everybody's attention went to Jordan as she took a huge leap in the air and then fell down.

"Yes, we all want to be just like Jordan," Belle replied with a snort.

"Back to work," Mrs. Booth commanded, which wiped the smile off Belle's face. Then Mrs. Booth looked at Shelby and me. She pulled at her light blue down vest, which matched with her earmuffs, gloves, and Belle's current skating outfit. "If I haven't made myself clear, I am extremely displeased there's another pairs team practicing here. I don't trust either of you."

Well, if I was being honest I didn't trust her, either. So there.

"Mom," Belle said in a tiny voice. "They're fine."

"They are not!" Mrs. Booth pointed at us. "They're a distraction."

Belle tried to speak over her loud mother. "You saw last night that they are at a different level."

Saw last night? What did that mean? Shelby and I weren't skating here last night.

I felt Shelby's elbow lightly jab me in the ribs.

No way. Mrs. Booth actually looked us up online!

Okay, she was definitely on our list of suspects.

"But I couldn't find any videos of you skating," Mrs. Booth remarked.

Uh-oh.

Shelby didn't miss a beat. "Oh, my parents have everything on video. And I mean everything. Would you like me to bring in their collection? It is rather large." What was Shelby doing? We didn't have any videos of us! At least that I knew of. "Of course, you'd have to listen to the constant blabbering from my parents during our routines. Unfortunately, they don't understand the nuances of skating. They can't differentiate between the jumps, so their commentary is quite pedestrian."

Mrs. Booth looked horrified that a parent didn't know every element of a figure skating program. She decided to turn to me. "You're only in the juvenile division?"

I was pretty sure we weren't even that high up, but it was what Shelby had written in those fake articles.

"That's right, Mrs. Booth," I replied. Then I decided to turn the tables and start asking her some questions. "Did you ever skate?"

Maybe that's what was going on. She was forcing her daughter to live out her own dreams and was going to take the competition down one by one. It didn't matter that Jordan didn't skate in pairs. Mrs. Booth wanted nobody skating with them.

It could be Mrs. Booth!

(So many suspects, so little time.)

Mrs. Booth ignored my question. "But you're what, six and ten?"

"Nine and eleven," Shelby corrected her.

"How are you not at the novice level? Belle has been skating since she was two."

Two? How was that even possible?

"Mom, none of this is going to help me win," Belle stated.

"Don't you mean *us?*" Douglas added. "Now come on, we've got to work on our jumps."

"Douglas is right. We need to focus on winning," Mrs. Booth replied. "Back to work, Belle!"

Belle skated to the center of the rink with Douglas, hand in hand.

Mrs. Booth began climbing the benches with her video camera. Interesting that she was accusing us of spying, when she could easily record Jordan or Aisha and leak the footage to their competition. Yeah, their main rivals were each other, but still.

"Are all athletes this dramatic?" Shelby asked.

"None that I've played with." *Thankfully.*

And if the last two days had shown me anything, it was that not only were figure skaters dramatic, they all appeared to be guilty.

CHAPTER 16

"WATSON!" SHELBY SNAPPED HER FINGERS AT ME. "ARE you paying attention?"

I nodded, but could hardly keep my eyes open. I'd been texting with my dad about meeting up later to do our Brooklyn Bridge walk. But first Shelby and I needed to crack this code.

We were in her bedroom after school with the ciphers spread on the floor. It seemed an impossible task for people fully rested. I'd been up for nearly twelve hours.

And we were going to have to do the same thing all over again tomorrow.

Being a figure skater was no joke.

Sir Arthur, Shelby's English bulldog, rested his chin on my leg, his eyes closed. *I know exactly how you feel, buddy.*

Shelby, however, had as much energy as ever. Anybody want to guess why?

She licked her fingers after eating her twelfth candy bar of the day. Yep, TWELFTH.

So much for her parents' ban. I think she was eating more sugar now, if that was even humanly possible.

Shelby got down to business. "Substitution ciphers have certain rules that have to be followed in order for someone to be able to understand them. Each of these figures represents a letter. During lunch, I broke it down to see any patterns."

I looked at the drawings and felt hopeless. I had no idea how we were going to do this.

Shelby continued, "E is the most used letter in the English language. In the first cipher there was one character that appeared the most—four times. I tried to crack it using E, but couldn't. I didn't have enough data. However, with the most recent cipher and the subsequent reply, there was one character that had been used six times. So let's assume this character is E," she said, pointing to the stick figure that, if it was facing us, had its left leg lifted in the air with the right arm raised and the left one pointing down. "I'll use dashes for the letters we don't know yet."

Shelby began writing in her notebook. Maybe we did have a chance to crack this thing after all. This was what she had.

Third cipher:
—–E– –– ––––E

–EE– –– ––––

Jordan's response:

–E–E–

So nothing. We had nothing.

"Okay, we have a break with Jordan's reply." Shelby circled -E-E-. "This could be one of three words: sever, lever, or, most likely, never. So now we know which characters are *N*, *R*, and *V*."

Shelby began writing so fast, I could hardly keep up.

Third cipher:

––E– –– ––R–E
NEE– –– ––––

Jordan's response:

NEVER

I felt deflated. That was it? We were never going to figure this out. NEVER. Or I guess I should say ♰♰♰♰♰.

Shelby didn't seem frustrated. She was practically giddy. "Let's fill in the other ciphers now that we know *E, N, R,* and *V.*"

First cipher:

––– –RE –––N– –– –––– –N– ––––

Second cipher:
---RE – ---ER

That's it? This was going to take forever.

"Okay, as you can see the second word in the first cipher is blank-*R-E*. Let's presume it's the word *are*. In this particular cipher, there is a three-letter word that precedes the word *are*. So this person is saying *blank are*. The most common three-letter word is *the*, but this particular word doesn't contain an *E*. After *the*, the most common three-letter words are: *and, for, but, you*—"

"YOU ARE!" I practically screamed.

Okay, I was getting into this. Maybe it wasn't impossible.

"If that's the case, we now have *A*, *Y*, *O*, and *U*." Shelby's head was down as she kept filling in letters.

First cipher:
YOU ARE –O–N– –O –A–– AN– –A––

Second cipher:
YOURE A –O–ER

Third cipher:
A–E– –– –OR–E
NEE– –O ––O–

Jordan's response:

NEVER

"And there is another three-letter word in that first cipher with the first two letters of *A-N*, so clearly that's *and*. So we also have *D*. Which now means that in the last cipher the third and fourth lines are as follows."

NEED –O ––O–

This person is telling Jordan that she needed . . . Jordan needed . . . "TO STOP!" It fit.

Shelby began filling in the blanks now that we had three more letters: *S*, *T*, and *P*.

First cipher:

YOU ARE –O–N– TO –A–– AND –A––

Second cipher:

YOURE A –OSER

Third cipher:

A–E– –S –ORSE
NEED TO STOP

Jordan's response:

NEVER

"Well," Shelby said through clenched teeth. "We now know which character is the letter *L*."

"We do?"

Shelby wrote down the phrase: *You're a loser.*

Oh. *Ouch.*

If we were right, that was what the second cipher said.

No wonder Jordan was having problems. That was mean. I didn't want to know what the others said now. Okay, I did, but, man. *Rude.*

Shelby took a step back from the cipher. "Well, the second word of the third cipher has to be *is*. With the letters *I* and *L*, we now have this."

First cipher:

YOU ARE –OIN– TO –ALL AND –AIL

Second cipher:

YOURE A LOSER

Third cipher:

A–EL IS –ORSE
NEED TO STOP

Jordan's response:

NEVER

We were almost there! I kept looking at the second line of the third cipher. Something is . . . a horse?

"Worse," Shelby filled in, but there weren't any more of the characters for *W*.

"What was worse?"

"Axel," Shelby stated. "The double axel was the only jump Jordan missed last year in competition. It cost her first place at sectionals."

"Okay, so the third cipher says *Axel is worse, need to stop.*" We already figured out Jordan's *never* reply a while ago. Now we just needed to figure out what the first cipher said. What started this whole thing. The note that got into Jordan's head. (Not like I could think of something worse than being called a loser.)

First cipher:

YOU ARE –OIN– TO –ALL AND –AIL

"You are . . . ," I started.

"Simple grammar dictates that the next word will end in *I-N-G*, and the first and last character are the same. So it says *you are going to . . .*"

Yeah, but going to what? What did this person tell Jordan that she was going to do that would have her so rattled?

Shelby took out a brand new piece of paper and wrote out the alphabet, crossing off the letters we knew. I couldn't believe it: we already had over a dozen letters.

Shelby studied the remaining letters. She sucked in a breath. She put her face down as she wrote something. "Watson, what's the worst thing a figure skater could do during a competition?"

"Forget their routine?" I'd watched a bunch of performances since we got this case and there were so many elements. I still couldn't tell a Salchow from a Lutz.

"No, something even worse."

Shelby held up the piece of paper.

YOU ARE GOING TO FALL AND FAIL

CHAPTER 17

"Morning!" Mom greeted me at the breakfast table. She had scrambled eggs in a pan on the stove.

"You're up!" I'd been leaving before she'd been awake.

"I missed you more than I will miss the sleep," she said before taking a sip of coffee.

"Thanks," I said as I helped myself to some eggs and grabbed a banana. "And sorry."

She arched her eyebrow. "Now what exactly do you have to be sorry about?"

I looked down at my food. "That I haven't seen you."

"John." Mom pulled her chair closer to me. "You have nothing to apologize for. I'm happy your father is here to see you."

"Really?" Then why did she always have to leave when he was around? Why couldn't the three of us hang out? But for some reason I didn't really want to know the answer to those questions so I kept quiet.

"Listen, the issues your father and I have are between him and me. You are the best thing that has ever happened to me and that's because of your father." She rubbed my cheeks with her thumb. "So, I hear you're having dinner at the Holmeses' tonight. I told your father to bring dessert to get on Shelby's good side."

"When did you talk to Dad?" I asked.

"We text all the time, John. I helped him plan this visit. We may not be together anymore, but we've got a very special boy to take care of. Although I hear his skating skills could use some work." She winked at me.

"Yeah, this case." I glanced at the clock. I had to be downstairs in two minutes.

"Go, go!" Mom said as she kissed me on the forehead. "Good luck today, Mr. Detective. And try to stay on your feet."

As we got out of the subway and headed west to Chelsea Piers, Shelby stopped walking. "I have a question for you."

"You have a question for me?" Usually Shelby just spouted information and told me what to look for. This was a totally welcomed change.

"Yes, didn't I just say that?" she snapped. "You seem to consider yourself an athlete."

And the compliments keep coming . . .

"So explain to me how someone can become so unraveled by a few messages. Aren't athletes supposed to be tough both physically and mentally?"

How could I explain to Shelby that most people didn't have impenetrable fortresses around their mind like she did? They cared what people thought. At least, I did. And so did everybody else I knew.

"Have you ever had a bully?" I asked.

And that was what this person was, right?

A bully.

Someone who said horrible things to a person to make themselves feel better. Someone who preyed on the vulnerable.

While I'd personally witnessed the snickers Shelby would sometimes get at school, it never seemed to get under her skin.

Shelby shook her head. "Nobody has had the nerve."

Fair point. Although . . . Shelby's abrupt behavior and sometimes taunting those not as smart as her (so, you know, *everybody*) could be considered bullying. It wasn't something I thought she did on purpose to hurt feelings, but still . . .

"See, I had a bully back in Maryland. When this guy, Donnie, arrived at the post, I did what I always did when a new person moved in: offered to show them around. It was how I wanted to be welcomed to a new post. Like my grandma always reminded me, 'Do unto others as you would have them do unto you.' Yeah, but Donnie apparently never had that lesson, as he was plain old mean. He called me names like 'loser' and 'short stack' since I hadn't had my growth spurt yet."

"There are many things one cannot be held accountable for, and your height is one of them," Shelby said with a shake of her head. "No shame in being on the shorter side. It especially helps with maneuvering around tight spaces."

"Yeah, but those names still stung. So, I started walking different ways to school to avoid him. Mom and Dad knew something was wrong, but I didn't want to tell on him."

This is the part of the story where I get ashamed. I should've said something, but I didn't.

I thought he'd eventually stop.

Spoiler alert: he didn't.

"What happened with this Donnie fellow?" Shelby asked with furrowed brows.

"Well, one day I was kicking around a ball in our backyard. It went in the road, where Donnie happened to be waiting. He took it and held it high above his head. 'Come on, man,' I had said to him. Then he replied, 'Naw, I don't think some stupid twerp like you should have this nice a ball.' Then he pushed me down."

Shelby's jaw clenched. I was kind of touched that she'd

be upset about something that had happened before she even knew me.

"Here's the good part: What Donnie didn't know was that my mom was in the living room. She heard everything and came running out. Seriously, the look on Donnie's face when Mom approached him was almost worth the weeks of his taunting. She took him by the collar and marched him home and had a talk with his folks. From then on, Donnie was the one avoiding me."

A smile spread on Shelby's face. "It is wise to not get on your mother's bad side. I am speaking from experience."

I let out a laugh. It's something people often say about Shelby. Hmm, maybe my mom and Shelby have a few things in common. You definitely don't want to cross either of them. And *I'm* speaking from experience on both fronts.

"Yeah, I didn't like it when Donnie pushed me, but what he said to me was worse. It was the first time I realized how hurtful words could be to someone. That is what's happening to Jordan. Athletes are strong, but competition can be as much of a mental game as a physical one. Once those words get planted—like 'loser'—it's hard to get them out of your mind. Sometimes it's easier to believe the worst about yourself."

Shelby was silent for a moment. When she spoke, it was

in a surprisingly soft voice. "Watson, do words people convey to you really hurt you?"

It wasn't the response I was expecting from her.

"They can."

She looked thoughtful. "Do I sometimes say something to you in a hurtful manner?"

Whoa. Was it possible Shelby Holmes was going to become self-aware?

"I mean, yeah, sometimes."

"I'd like specific examples of said behavior," she stated with a sniff.

"Ah." Where do I begin? "You get really short with me when I don't know something, and you sometimes say things about my abilities in front of others. I'm still learning."

"Neither of those statements are a specific example, now are they, Watson? And how are you going to learn if I don't point out when you are wrong. In fact, I do not mention every occasion you're incorrect as there are only so many hours in a day."

"Right there!" I pointed at her.

"What?" Shelby genuinely seemed confused. "What word—*exactly*—did I say that would be classified as bullying?"

"It's more of how you say it."

"Oh, so it's the tone of my voice." She then put on her sweet Roberta voice. "Is this better?"

"Never mind." I started walking faster. I should've known better. I mean, really, there was sometimes no point in trying to reason with her.

But as we waited at a crossing light, Shelby said something I never expected from her.

"I'm sorry, Watson. I'll try to be more aware of my tone and vocabulary." She then patted me on the back.

I was so stunned. I stood there with my mouth open, even after we had the walk signal.

I did it! She was learning about being a better (and hopefully more tolerable) friend! Miracles can happen!

Shelby turned around as she crossed the street. "Not the time to be resting on either your laurels or the corner, Watson."

Or maybe not.

As we approached the Sky Rink, a knot began forming in my stomach. I hoped Jordan's bully was just going to stick to leaving notes.

I didn't want to think what this person was going to do if they decided to take it a step further.

But as we opened the door to the rink, it was clear there was something going on.

"Get your head in the game, Belle!" Belle's mom shouted as we entered the rink. She was wearing yellow head to toe and had a huge cup of coffee in her hand. She kept nervously pacing back and forth. "You need to do it again. This time *without* falling. You have three days to get your act together."

Well, Mrs. Booth certainly fit the profile of a bully.

Over on the other ice, Jordan was skating fast. Really fast. And taking huge jumps and landing them, only to jump again.

She was staying on her feet!

"No!" Belle's mom shouted as my attention went back to her. "What has gotten into you?"

I looked back to the ice and saw . . . Belle?

It had to be Belle because she was skating with Douglas and it was the person getting wrath from Belle's mom, but . . .

Shelby and I exchanged a look. Sure, it was only our third day at the rink, but I think I remembered what Belle looked like. Or at least that she had dark hair and now was blond. Did she dye her hair? Or was she wearing a blond wig?

No, that didn't make sense. Why would someone wear a wig while skating? No way would that thing stay on.

Belle was flying right over to her mom, her teeth clenched. She tore a wig off her head, and then started ripping bobby pins out of her hair.

What was going on? Could one thing about this case start making sense?

"Maybe this ridiculous thing is getting in my way." Belle threw it at her mom. It landed near Shelby's feet.

Sergi skated over. "No wig. We must focus on elements."

Belle narrowed her eyes at her mom. "Told you."

"I think you look more cohesive with Douglas if you have blond hair." Mrs. Booth picked up the wig.

"No more distractions," Sergi shouted. "No more autographs! No more watching videos! We skate! Skate only way to win!"

Mrs. Booth sighed, but sat down on the bench nearest the entrance.

"Stop with the shouting!" Tatiana yelled to Sergi. "You biggest distraction here!"

Between the glass that separated the rinks, the two former skating partners and couple glared at each other for a few uncomfortable moments before bringing their attention back to their skaters.

Yikes. The tension was intense.

Shelby walked over to Mrs. Booth, her eyes focused on the wig. "Excuse me, are you going to use that?"

Mrs. Booth did a double take, not realizing we were

there and had witnessed the fight between her and her daughter. And then Sergi and Tatiana. "But you have such lovely red hair."

"Why, thank you so much. But you never know when you'll need to have blond hair, right?" Shelby said with an innocent smile.

(More like, Shelby never knew when she needed to go undercover as a blond.)

Mrs. Booth stared at the limp wig in her hand. "Sure. Have it. The things we try in order to ensure a victory."

Shelby sat down next to Mrs. Booth and started to tie her skates. "May I inquire as to why you wanted your daughter to be blond? She has a nice shade of black hair."

"It was a silly idea I had." Mrs. Booth shook her head. "It was nothing."

"I'm sure it was something, since regionals are approaching. We skaters need every advantage to score high."

"That was exactly what I was thinking!" Mrs. Booth's jaw was set stubbornly. "I was looking at old footage of Douglas and Jordan skating. They were such a dynamic pair. I simply noticed that one thing that made it hard to take your eyes off them was that they seemed to fit so well with each other. It was like they were born to skate together."

I looked over at a blond Douglas and then over to a blond Jordan.

So Mrs. Booth wanted her daughter to be more like Jordan. I wondered what else she was willing to do to get her daughter to win. Like, oh, I don't know . . . leave bullying ciphers to mess with Jordan's mind.

But if I was being honest, the only person who had the biggest motivation was Aisha.

I had to think clearly. Aisha didn't seem like a bully, but what did I know?

Maybe Shelby had a point about not making a case personal. It was hard for me to see Aisha as an evil culprit. She was the opposite of what I pictured this bullying person to be. But maybe . . . that was exactly what she wanted us to think.

Mrs. Booth took her video camera and walked to the top of the bleachers to get the best view of the rink. Tatiana skated over to Shelby and me. She shook her head. "No message today."

No message? What did *that* mean? What were we supposed to do *now*?

Shelby stood up. "Well, Julian. I guess it's time we skate."

Oh no. Not that. Anything but that.

CHAPTER 18

Progress!

Well, sort of.

Are you ready for this? Shelby and I had managed to remain upright for *fifteen minutes* as we skated around the rink.

Yep. Fifteen whole minutes.

Not bad. Not bad at all.

Especially since Jordan wasn't so lucky. She didn't fall with every jump, but she did fall. A lot. The only time I came close to landing on my butt was when Jordan skated by us so fast, it startled me.

Shelby and I skated back toward the bench to rest. I couldn't believe it wasn't even seven o'clock yet.

Mrs. Booth was laughing as we sat down. "I guess I should apologize."

Okaaay. Where was *that* coming from?

"Clearly you aren't competition."

Duh. That was what we were trying to tell her.

"What I can't figure out is why Tatiana is wasting her time with you when she has Jordan. All you did was skate around. You can't jump? Spin? Something is off about you two." She wagged her finger at us.

"I'm nursing an injury so I have to take it easy," Shelby replied through gritted teeth.

Hey, that was the excuse I wanted to use on our first day! No fair!

"I'm going to do a circle to make sure a cipher wasn't missed," Shelby whispered to me. "I'll be right back."

I sat there and watched the other skaters. Mrs. Booth had a point: we were nowhere near as good as her daughter. Or anybody else. But we'd only been skating for a few days. The fact that I stayed upright in itself was a victory. I didn't want to fall in front of Aisha. Or any of them, really.

Aisha skated over and got out of the rink as music cued up for Douglas and Belle's routine. Mrs. Booth hovered with her video camera as the pair began spinning around.

"They're really good," Aisha said as she sat down next to me.

"Yeah," I replied.

Why was I nervous being near her? Was it because she was our lead suspect?

Yep, that was what I was going with.

She could be guilty.

Douglas and Belle finished their routine and we all clapped, except for Mrs. Booth. "You wobbled on your camel, Belle!"

Always a critic.

Douglas seemed frustrated. "You need to hold on to me tighter when we spin. I could feel you losing your grip. Jordan always locked her fingers when she did it. Maybe she can show you?"

"Oh yes!" Mrs. Booth clapped her hands excitedly. "What a wonderful idea! Let's ask Jordan for some pointers when she's done today."

Belle hung her head as she got off the ice.

Aisha stood up and started to stretch. "Well, it's my turn. Wish me luck."

"Good luck," I repeated, but I wanted to say something more. "And, you know, you're like, um, also really good."

Aisha's entire face lit up. "Thank you! It's been a lot of work, but I love it."

"I can tell." Not like I'd been spending lots of time looking at her or whatever, but she kind of came alive when she was on the ice. The only time I'd seen anybody that happy about what they were doing was when Shelby was inhaling candy.

"Thanks, you're so sweet!" She then reached down and gave me a hug.

Bullies didn't give good hugs, did they? (Please say no.)

Aisha returned to the rink as Mrs. Booth continued to give Belle an earful about her performance, which I thought was really good. But yet again, what did I know? (About anything apparently.)

Shelby came back. "Nothing," she reported.

Should we be relieved or worried that there weren't any messages?

Shelby took a quick look at me and shook her head.

"What?" I asked.

"Fraternizing with a suspect," she said with a twitch of her nose.

"What are you—"

She pointed to my left shoulder, which had glitter on it from Aisha's hug.

"I was just being nice," I defended myself.

"Oh, I'm sure."

You know what, I take it back. Shelby *was* a bully. I mean, she was only telling the truth, but I didn't like her attitude. I could be nice to people and still be a detective. She should maybe try it, for a change.

Jordan skated over to the side of the rink, in front of us. She gave us a little nod as she picked up her water bottle.

Shelby stood up and narrowed her eyes.

"Don't drink that!" Shelby said quietly as she took the bottle from Jordan's hand.

"What are you doing?" Jordan asked loudly.

Tatiana skated over. The three of us watched Shelby as she swirled the water around Jordan's bottle, then twisted off the lid and sniffed it. Shelby placed the bottle back down. "Don't touch," she said under her breath. "Pretend that we're having a team meeting or whatever it is you do."

Tatiana nodded as she clapped her hands. "Okay, we talk schedule," she said loudly.

"What's going on?" Jordan asked as she tried to grab her water bottle, but stopped when she saw the glare from Shelby.

"Have you had a sip of this yet?"

"No. What's the big deal?" Jordan put the bottle up to her lips.

"I would advise you don't drink that unless you want to spend the majority of the day in the bathroom."

"What?" all three of us asked.

The color drained from Jordan's already pale face. "What?" she repeated.

"Someone put an oily substance in this water," Shelby whispered as she studied the bottle carefully. "I need to do some testing, but I'm fairly certain I know what it is. It would make you a little sick, but wouldn't do any permanent damage."

No permanent damage? I don't think that was making anybody feel better. I certainly felt a little sick to *my* stomach knowing that the person had moved from notes to sabotage. And I wasn't even the person they were targeting!

"How do you know all of this?" Jordan asked.

Shelby examined her for a minute, then sighed. "Well, I think it's time we dispense with the charade." She then turned to me. "Watson, what's going to be our biggest obstacle in finding the person who tampered with this?"

"Who's Watson?" Jordan asked, looking between the two of us.

I couldn't believe Shelby used my real name, but I guess she had decided that Jordan needed to know our real identities.

"Watson?" Shelby repeated. "Biggest obstacle?"

Ah, the fact that anybody here could've done it? But no. There had to be something special about this case and where we were. I quickly examined everybody in the rink. We all had one thing in common. And one thing that would make identifying a criminal difficult.

"Gloves," I replied. Shelby wouldn't be able to dust for fingerprints.

Once again, gloves were proving to be an issue for us. Who knew?

"Exactly." Shelby produced tweezers from inside her skate. First the ciphers and now tweezers? What else did she have in there? I was used to her backpack being stuffed with every possible item you could need while solving a case. I had no idea how she fit her foot in that boot with everything else she apparently had stashed in there.

"Hello! What's this?" Shelby said as she took the tweezers and picked up something from near the lid. It was a black piece of fuzz. "Who's wearing black gloves?"

I looked around. "Douglas . . ." I flinched. "Aisha . . ." Sergi had red gloves while Belle and her mom had yellow gloves that had some sort of snowflake pattern.

"And me," Jordan said as she waved her black-clad fingers at us. "Would you please explain what is— Hey!" she protested as Shelby plucked a fiber from Jordan's gloves.

Shelby held both pieces up to the light. One had a bit of gray in it and was thicker than the other.

"Different gloves," Shelby stated. "Your fiber is made from merino wool, while the other is alpaca."

Jordan's forehead was creased. "Can someone please explain what's going on here?"

"Jordan, I think it's time we have a little talk."

CHAPTER 19

"I DON'T UNDERSTAND WHAT'S GOING ON." JORDAN PACED back and forth in Tatiana's office. "Who are you again?"

"I'm John Watson and this is Shelby Holmes. We're here to help find the person who is sending you the ciphers," I explained.

"What's a cipher?" Jordan asked with a flip of her ponytail.

"It's the messages you've been getting," Shelby stated flatly.

"Oh, those." Her eyes darted around the room, not willing to make eye contact with either of us.

"And we aren't figure skaters," I clarified.

Jordan stopped walking and started laughing. She covered her mouth with her hand. "Sorry! Really, I figured you weren't figure skaters." She turned to Tatiana. "I was wondering why you were bringing in another team so close to regionals. I thought you were giving up on me."

"Never!" Tatiana rubbed Jordan's shoulders. "I hired them for help. You no talk to me. You too upset."

"I know, but it's silly trash-talking. I shouldn't let it affect me. If I want to make it to the Olympics someday, I should get used to this. I promise I'll focus harder. I will land that double axel. I won't let words get in my head."

"Yeah, but words can hurt," I said. "I've been bullied before and it's not fun. I'd started thinking that what this person was saying about me was true, and well, you can say that it's silly, but it clearly upset you."

"Of course, it does," Jordan admitted. Tatiana pulled her into a hug. "I'm sorry I didn't tell you. I didn't want you to think I was weak."

Same with me. I didn't want my parents to think I couldn't handle a few mean comments, but I felt so much better after they found out. Who was I protecting by keeping it inside? Nobody but the bully.

And now, with Jordan, it wasn't simply words.

"Listen, this has gotten a little beyond trash-talking. That stuff in your water. It could get dangerous." I glanced over at her bottle. If you looked closely, you could see that there was an oily substance in it.

Jordan pulled apart from Tatiana and wiped away a tear. "Okay. You're right. I can't ignore this anymore. What do you need to know?"

Shelby walked up to Jordan and started circling her. "How do you know about the code? Who taught it to you?"

"We came up with it at camp years ago."

"I presume this is The Mosley Academy you attend every summer," Shelby clarified to a surprised Jordan. "Who is *we*?"

Jordan glanced nervously at Tatiana. "Well, it wasn't anything big. We wanted a way to talk without our coaches knowing."

"Again," Shelby said, her patience wearing thin, "who is we?"

"Me and Douglas."

It was Douglas! (Not Aisha! YES!)

"Don't get too excited, Watson," Shelby replied dryly. "Are you the only two who know it?"

Jordan shook her head. "No. The first year it was just the two of us. But then the next summer we shared it with some of the other campers. We wanted to find ways to sneak out and eat candy and pizza or stay up late. They're very strict about our diet and sleep at camp."

"That sounds awful," Shelby said with a look of actual pity on her face. She didn't really have empathy for anybody, except if you took away a person's sugar.

"It's what you have to do to become a champion," Jordan replied as she looked at Tatiana. "Besides, I know who's sending me the messages."

"You do?" Tatiana asked. "Why not you tell me?"

"It's pretty obvious: Aisha."

UGH.

Shelby tilted her head. "Why would you say that? Did you see her doing it?"

"No, but we have this rivalry. She was at camp with us so she knows the code."

No, no, no, NO!

"And, okay," Jordan said with a scowl. "We've maybe had some issues in the past. What kills me is that I let her get into my head. Her plan is working."

Shelby didn't seem satisfied with that answer, which gave me a small sliver of hope. "So Aisha is your only competitor who knows the cipher?"

"There are others, but none who live in New York."

"Can you provide me with a list of everybody who has the code?"

"Sure."

Shelby approached one of the photos in the office. It was of Jordan and Douglas from two years ago. They were on the ice, either getting ready to start a routine or finishing it, and they were both looking at each other and smiling. "How did Douglas take it when you decided to go solo?"

"He was upset." Jordan began wringing her hands. "I felt awful about it at the time, but now he has a great partner with Belle. Look, Douglas would never do this. Ever. He's practically my brother and one of my closest friends. I've been skating with him since I could walk. Our parents thought we should skate together, but then I started to . . ."

There was a silence in the room until Tatiana stated what Jordan seemed too embarrassed or guilty to say. "She better skater. He hold her back."

Jordan's cheeks became flush. "It was rough for a while. Both Douglas and Sergi felt betrayed, but everything's cool now. It's been over a year."

Shelby didn't seem very convinced. Neither did I.

"Plus, what would Douglas have to gain if I dropped out?" Jordan added. "He's not my competition. Aisha is."

"You are underestimating the grudge of a boy scorned," Shelby stated.

Jordan shook her head. "Not Douglas. He's not like that. So, are you going to talk to Aisha?"

"We have several suspects we'll be speaking with."

"I appreciate your help and all, but I really think that'll be a waste of your time."

Shelby smirked. "I'll be the judge of that."

Jordan stood up. "Okay. Can I get back to skating?"

Shelby gestured toward the door. "By all means, but you need to proceed with caution. This person has gone beyond words now."

"You mean *Aisha* has gone beyond."

It looked like Jordan was not going to drop her Aisha suspicion. My mind flashed back to all the times I'd seen Jordan off the rink. She was always hanging with Douglas and Belle. She never seemed to look at Aisha, let alone talk to her. It made sense she'd simply assume it was Aisha. But what if it wasn't?

Jordan paused before she walked out of the room. "But if you did catch her, she'd probably get kicked out of the US Figure Skating Association."

"Just like what happened to the person who messed with her skates last year?" Shelby said with a smirk.

Jordan's jaw went slack. "That was never proven." Her voice was barely audible.

"One last question," Shelby said. "Anybody else in the rink know the code? Sergi? Belle?"

"Belle's mom?" I added.

Jordan sighed. "No. The coaches didn't know we even had a code, but I guess they do now. Belle was too young and wasn't at the camp back then. Listen, I have three days to nail my routines, so I really have to get back out on the ice. I hope you find the girl doing this, but I can only control my performance." Jordan shrugged her shoulders before leaving with Tatiana.

"What do you think?" I asked.

"If Jordan is telling us the truth, we have a couple people to remove from the suspect list."

"So it's either Douglas or . . ." I couldn't bring myself to say it.

But Shelby had no trouble finishing the thought for me. "Aisha."

I dragged my feet back to the rink where everybody was skating like usual. My attention focused on Douglas and Aisha. One of them was responsible for this. I sank down on the bench in defeat.

"Excuse me." Mrs. Booth walked over.

What now?

"Where did you get that?" She was pointing to something in my hand. I was holding one of the ciphers. I forgot to put it away before we walked out.

"I—I—" I stuttered.

"How do you know those drawings?"

Wait a second. How did *she* know these drawings?

"We learned it at The Mosley Academy," Shelby replied quickly as she sat down next to me. "Are you familiar?"

Mrs. Booth nodded. "Yes. Belle keeps getting these messages." She grabbed the sheet and studied it. "I don't know what it means, though."

WHAT?

Belle was also being bullied?

"It's just something we do for fun," Shelby replied coolly. "Come along, Julian. Best to get back to practice."

Well, this day kept getting better.

Shelby took my hand as we went back out on the ice. "Oh, Watson, this just got interesting."

Interesting? Didn't she mean *confusing?*

Because the more we found out about this case, the less sense it made.

CHAPTER
20

HEY, SO—FUN FACT: YOU CAN APPARENTLY FALL ASLEEP standing up.

Yep. True story.

"Watson?" Jason's voice jolted me awake as I was leaning half-in, half-out of my locker after school. "You okay?"

I blinked a few times to wake myself up. "Yeah."

But was I really okay? I was exhausted. Even though the school day was over, I still had plans to hang out with Dad before we had dinner with Shelby's family.

There didn't seem to be enough time in the day.

"Do you need my notes from English?" Jason asked. "You were staring off like a zombie or something." He laughed.

"Yeah, that would be great."

Because on top of everything, I still had homework. Couldn't forget that.

This case couldn't end soon enough.

Now that we knew Belle was also getting notes, it had to be Douglas. Who else would have problems with Jordan, his former partner, and Belle, his current one? Although Belle hadn't been acting any differently. It was her mom who seemed to be distracting her more than anything.

But I didn't really know Belle. Maybe she had been frazzled?

The most important question I had was: What now? How were Shelby and I going to finally solve this thing?

I looked around the hallway for Shelby, but couldn't find her.

"Here," Jason said as he took a photo of his notebook. "I'll text you."

"Thanks, man."

My stomach growled. These long days had made me extra hungry. After the "Moira Incident," both Mom and Shelby had made sure I always have food, water, and juice on me at all times.

I took out my backpack and unzipped the front pocket to grab a bag of almonds. A slip of paper came out.

Someone left me a note?

I unfolded it to find this written on notebook paper:

A new cipher.

For me.

"Whoa, is that one of your codes?" Jason asked.

"Yeah," I replied as I sat down on the floor and took out a copy of our notes with the decryption.

And, of course, the first letter was new. But I started working on the rest of the code. So far I had: -EET -E AT. We didn't have the letter *M* yet, so I had to deduce that I was being told to meet someone at . . . My hands worked overtime.

Jason sat down next to me and watched as I broke the code.

MEET ME AT SALS FOUR

"What's Sals Four?" I asked aloud. Was it some kind of store?

Jason took the piece of paper. "I think it means that you're supposed to meet someone at Sal's at four o'clock."

"Oh," I replied, feeling foolish since I was supposed to be the detective. (I was also on very little sleep.) "Right. Thanks."

"Is it safe for you to go there by yourself?" Jason asked. "You want backup?"

"It's fine. It's from Shelby."

Shelby was the one who had the code. She probably made up a new character for *M*. Shelby liked going to Sal's. Who else would've sent me the cipher? But why didn't she just tell me when I saw her at lunch or in Mr. Crosby's class? Or text me?

Because it's Shelby. She doesn't make anything easy.

Oh, yeah. That.

"Well, I better go," I said to Jason as I grabbed my jacket and headed out of the building. If I was done at Sal's before four thirty, I might have enough time to do my homework before Dad showed up at five. I hoped. "Talk to you later."

My feet moved slowly during the dozen blocks to Sal's. At least there was pizza in my future. I started thinking about the case. Shelby must've figured something out.

As much as I wanted to interrogate Belle and her mom about the ciphers Belle had been receiving, Shelby didn't want them to know we were aware of Jordan's notes or blow our cover. But regionals were in three days. We had to figure out how to get Douglas to confess. Or at least catch him in a trap.

I walked into Sal's right at four o'clock, but a quick scan showed that I was the first one to arrive.

Weird. Shelby was always early.

I slid into a booth right as my phone buzzed in my bag. It was a text from Shelby, probably telling me the unthinkable and that she was, for the first time in the history of modern timekeeping, late.

Talked to Jason. Watson, that cipher wasn't from me.

WHAT?!?!

If Shelby wasn't the one who sent me the note, who did?

All of a sudden I felt sick to my stomach.

There was only one person sending ciphers. They were up to no good.

And it looked like I was their next target.

"Watson!" I jumped as Sal called out my name. "So good to see you. You want some cheesy garlic bread?"

I automatically nodded even though I was no longer hungry.

I had to get out of there right away. Before it was too late.

"You came." I froze as a voice sounded behind me. "I wasn't sure if you would."

No. NO. NO!

WHY DOES THIS KEEP HAPPENING TO ME?

I, John Howard Watson, am the most gullible human being alive.

Slowly, I turned around and there she was. The person who sent me the cipher. The one who lured me into her trap.

Aisha.

CHAPTER 21

AISHA SLID INTO THE SEAT ACROSS FROM ME, A SMILE ON HER face.

She doesn't look like a bully or criminal mastermind.

Yeah, but I'd been wrong before.

She smiled at me. It was a warm smile. A nice smile. A really pretty smile.

Ugh. I was in so much trouble and all I could think of was how cute Aisha looked. It was the first time I'd seen her out of her skating clothes. Her hair was down and she had on jeans and a pink fuzzy sweater that hung off one shoulder. She looked like a regular girl.

Not at all like a guilty culprit.

Trouble. Trouble. Trouble.

"Watson!" Sal approached us, his arms stretched out. "What can I get your lovely friend?"

Aisha didn't even look at the menu. "Water and a small salad, dressing on the side, please." She then leaned in toward me and said, "After regionals, I'm coming here and eating an entire pizza by myself."

I was mute. I didn't know what to say. Or what to do.

"Who's Watson?" she asked.

"Ah . . . ," I murmured.

"Look, I'm sorry to be so secretive about meeting you. There's just a lot of pressure on me right now. I overheard Mrs. Booth mentioning she saw you guys with the secret code. So I decided to take a shot and ask you to meet me outside the rink. You know, to get to know you better."

I simply nodded. My phone in my backpack kept buzzing. I hadn't had a chance to respond to Shelby. I needed to tell her that Aisha was the one sending the ciphers. And that she had me cornered.

No. I could do this on my own. I needed to use this moment to interrogate her. I remembered all the things Shelby had told me about questioning a witness. It was best to do it when they didn't even realize they were a suspect. It gave them a false sense of security. Here we were, just two skaters at a pizza place.

"My parents would kill me if they knew I was here." Aisha tucked one of her twists behind her ear.

Sal put a basket of cheesy garlic bread in front of us. I needed a couple more minutes to figure out a plan so I took a huge bite of bread. The hot cheese scalded the roof of my mouth.

"Hot, hot," I called out as I took a large sip of water.

Aisha put her nose close to the bread and took a deep breath. "It smells so good. I guess one little bite won't hurt." She picked up a piece and put it on a napkin. "But I'll wait for it to cool."

Okay, think, Watson. You've always known how to talk to people. I simply had to ask her some open-ended questions. It was best to let someone talk and talk. The more a person spoke, the better the chance to get them to say something incriminating.

"Your parents are strict?" I asked.

Aisha slumped back into the booth. "Yes. Don't get me wrong, I'm the one who wants to skate. Being in the rink is one of the few times I really feel like me. But it's expensive and my parents have had to take on extra jobs. They've been making sacrifices for me so I need to be focused on skating one hundred percent."

I nodded, but didn't reply because I wanted her to continue. Silence makes people uncomfortable so hopefully she'd keep talking and something would slip.

(See, Aisha wasn't the only one who could set a trap.)

Sal placed a salad in front of Aisha and she started to pick at it with a fork. "I usually am focused, but right before a competition I want distraction. If I get too freaked out before a skate, I overthink things. I just need to go in there on Saturday and do what I know I can do. What I've been trained to do."

I nodded yet again. So Aisha wanted a distraction. What better way to distract yourself than by sending cryptic messages to the competition?

But why to Belle? Maybe she didn't want to share a rink with anybody? Jordan didn't have to.

"What about you?" Aisha asked as she took a bite of a lettuce leaf.

What about *me*?

I needed to get her to confess and to find out what her endgame was. Would she stop harassing Jordan after regionals, or was this only the beginning?

"Hey," I said, knowing that I had to get it out there. "I heard a rumor the other day about you and Jordan."

Aisha froze for a moment before setting her fork down. "What rumor?"

I wanted to make this as vague as possible. "About a shoelace."

She grimaced. "Yes. I don't know for sure if it was Jordan, but it wouldn't be the first time she got creative when it came to winning."

Hold on. It couldn't be possible it was Jordan sending

herself ciphers and doing all of this to make Aisha look guilty. Could it?

But Jordan wasn't the one who came to us, Tatiana did. And Jordan didn't seem to think this was a big deal. She said it was all in her head.

Which was *exactly* something a guilty person would say.

"Like what?" I pressed. I needed to know what else Jordan was capable of.

"Well, there was another skater who bunked with her at world's two years ago, Katrina. The skirt of her costume mysteriously went missing right before her long program. I've learned to keep everything locked up. Or at least give it to my parents or Sergi."

"So Jordan is your main rival?" While I already knew that was true, I wanted to hear how Aisha would describe their relationship. And how she would react.

I looked into her big brown eyes.

(Trouble. Trouble. Trouble.)

She shifted her gaze away from me and shrugged. "I guess. But I never looked at it like this person is the enemy. At the end of the day, it's me out on the ice. I have to do the best routine I can. It's not anybody's fault if I fall except my own. Well, unless they tamper with my laces, but we got that fixed in time. And did whoever told you that also mention I wound up in first place, even with the last-minute dramatics?"

"Everything good, Watson?" Sal came over.

"Yeah, great, thanks!"

Aisha's brows furrowed. "Why does he keep calling you Watson?"

"Ah, it's a nickname." Which was technically true, thank you very much.

The front door burst open and Shelby came into the restaurant. Her face was flushed and she was trying to steady her breath. She must've run all the way here.

"Roberta!" Aisha said right as Sal came over to Shelby.

"My favorite customer!" he exclaimed as he patted Shelby on the head. "Have you come for my special Nutella pizza?"

Aisha's eyes got wide. "They have Nutella pizza here?"

Shelby studied us, a smile on her face as she saw Aisha. "Yes. I've had them recently add it to the menu."

Ah. Sal's didn't have a dessert menu so Shelby's parents probably never thought about coming in here and telling Sal that Shelby was off sweets. While I admired Shelby's parents for trying, they had to know she'd find a way to get around it. I mean, honestly . . .

"A large?" Sal asked as he looked at us.

"Oh, I can't," Aisha said as she patted her stomach. "As much as I want to."

"Yeah, me too," I replied.

"Diet?" Aisha asked.

"Diabetes."

"Yes, a large," Shelby replied as she looked at Aisha. "I'm going to need a lot of sugar for this."

Sal laughed. "Whatever you need, Shelby!"

"Shelby?" Aisha asked. "Why does he—"

Shelby reached her hand out to me. "Let me see it."

"See what? What's going on?" Aisha's eyes kept darting between us.

I pulled out the cipher Aisha had slipped into my bag. Shelby held it up to the light, then put her nose inches away from it.

"Why is she . . . ?" Aisha shook her head. "Is there a problem that I gave you a note? Is there something going on between you two?"

"No!" both Shelby and I protested.

I mean, yeah, Shelby was my best friend and all, but that was it.

Plus, let's be real, I had enough problems in my life without adding girls to the mix.

Shelby put the paper on the table. "Well, Watson, I have good news."

Good news? It was about time!

"Aisha isn't the perpetrator."

CHAPTER 22

SHE WASN'T?

I wasn't the only one confused.

"Perpetrator?" Aisha asked with her hands on her hips. "What exactly do you think I did?"

Shelby ignored her. "Look." She took out one of the ciphers Jordan received. "See how Aisha's handwriting is looser and larger than that of the person sending Jordan these notes."

I looked at both ciphers in my hand. Side by side, it was clear that they weren't from the same person.

So who was sending the ciphers?

(It had to be Douglas now, right?)

"Can someone please tell me what's going on?" Aisha looked at me. "Julian? Or is it Watson?"

Busted.

Shelby sat next to me in the booth. "I must speak bluntly with you, Aisha. Can you be trusted?"

Aisha looked offended. "Can *you* trust *me*? I'm not the one with different names or talking about handwriting or . . ." It was like a lightbulb went on over her head. "Are you guys even skaters?" She started laughing lightly. "I mean, it was clear you both needed a lot of work, but I'd assumed Tatiana was doing something for charity."

Ouch. We weren't that bad.

(Okay, we were.)

Shelby's reply was to shove a large piece of cheesy garlic bread into her mouth.

So, it seemed like it was up to me to tell her the truth.

I glanced around the crowded restaurant. I guessed it was safe to come clean here. I mean, everybody knew Shelby. And a lot of them knew me now, too.

"What?" Aisha looked around, paranoid. "You're making me nervous. Who are you guys? What's going on?"

"Okay, can we trust you?" I asked again, quietly so no one could hear us.

Aisha paused for a moment. "Yes, you can trust me. However, I'm starting to think I can't trust you."

Fair enough.

"My name is John Watson and this is Shelby Holmes."

Shelby nodded as Sal put a huge pizza covered in chocolate sauce and something white and fluffy in front of her. My teeth hurt just looking at it.

"We have dinner in two hours," I reminded Shelby.

"Exactly," she replied as she dived into the sugary concoction.

My attention went back to Aisha who looked in shock. "Okay, John and Shelby. But I still don't understand why you'd lie. Why were you pretending to be skaters?"

"We didn't lie. We're . . . undercover. We're detectives, and someone has been sending Jordan these messages. So Tatiana came to us to help find out who was doing it."

"You two?" She pointed at us with a look of disbelief. "You're detectives."

Shelby groaned. I had to admit that I was getting annoyed that no one could ever believe that yes, we were detectives. I mean, Shelby's face was currently covered in chocolate, but anybody who talked to her for more than a minute could tell that she was something special.

Aisha started gathering her things. "I don't believe this."

"Ask around," Shelby said with a full mouth. "You can start with Sal here. He'll tell you all about what I can do. Watson has proven to be quite competent on several occasions."

Oh boy. I had to remind myself that to Shelby Holmes, that was a huge compliment.

"Okay, so let's say I believe you." Aisha put her stuff back down. "Jordan's been getting messages? What kind of messages?"

162

"Someone's been telling her these mean things like she's going to fall and that she's a failure."

Aisha began nodding slowly. "So that's why she hasn't been skating like herself lately." Then her jaw dropped open. "Wait. You thought that *I* was the one sending her messages?"

She looked hurt and she was staring right at me.

"You were one of our suspects, yes," Shelby replied. "You knew the code. You had access to the rink."

"But it's not me! I would never—" Aisha's shoulders sank. "Who else is a suspect?"

"Those who know the code, you and Douglas," Shelby replied.

"And Belle," Aisha added.

"Belle knows the code?" I asked.

"Of course," Shelby answered for Aisha. "Her mom saw her with the code, so she has to be able to read it."

"Oh, yeah, her mom said Belle had been getting notes, too."

"No." Shelby licked sugar from her fingers. "We can only imply from what Mrs. Booth communicated that Belle has been seen with these messages. She never saw her receive them. That was a presumption Mrs. Booth made. When solving a case, it's dangerous to jump to conclusions before all the facts are available."

"We've been using the code for a few months," Aisha commented. "We wanted to have a way to talk behind Sergi's back. He can be really hard on us. It was innocent, just a way for us to vent. But then Sergi discovered the key."

"Sergi knows the cipher?" I asked.

"Yeah," Aisha said, like it wasn't this huge deal.

Because who would benefit the most from having Tatiana's only client not place at regionals?

Her ex-partner.

"Whoa," I said aloud. I put my head in my hands and leaned my forehead on the table. Every time I thought we were coming close to figuring this case out, there'd be another curve ball.

"Is he okay?" Aisha asked.

Shelby snorted. "He'll be fine."

There was a nudge of my shoulder. I looked up to see Shelby smiling, which was never a good sign.

"Come on, Watson. I'd say that the day would get better but we still have the matter of dinner with my family."

With that, Shelby helped herself to a second slice of Nutella pizza.

There was no way this day could get any more confusing or longer.

At least I hoped.

CHAPTER 23

"SORRY!" I TOLD DAD AS HE WALKED UP THE FLIGHT OF stairs to the apartment.

"It's okay," he replied. "Schoolwork is important. I get to see you now and that's all that counts."

I hated having to cancel on Dad before dinner, but I had to get my homework done since I knew I'd crash after.

"Oh," Dad said as I shut the door to the apartment behind me.

"You're going to love Shelby's parents. They're the complete opposite of her," I said, trying to distract him from the fact that I was instructed by Mom to take Dad straight up to the Holmeses'.

But by the look he gave the door, he knew what was going on.

We started up the stairs to the Holmeses' floor.

He cleared his throat. "Look, son, I wanted to—"

"Good evening," Shelby greeted us at the top of the

stairs. "I thought I'd save you the torture of having to endure going through Michael to gain entrance."

"Hey, Shelby!" Dad exclaimed. "And Michael is your brother, right?"

"Unfortunately. You can't disagree with DNA results."

Dad laughed nervously as we walked into their apartment. "Yeah, I guess."

"Martin!" Shelby's dad approached him. "So nice to meet you. We're big fans of your son here."

"We certainly are," Mrs. Holmes said as she appeared behind her husband.

Shelby plopped down on the couch with a sulk. I couldn't contain my smile. I liked Shelby's parents. They were nice and friendly, and, you know, behaved like regular people.

"I brought you dessert," Dad said as he handed them a box from Levain Bakery.

Shelby perked up, while her parents exchanged a look. "Why, that was awfully gracious of you."

Yeah, I should've told Dad not to bring dessert, even though Mom suggested it. But when we went to Levain the other day, he insisted on getting cookies for dinner. Mom even gave me permission to eat half of one (which honestly, is like two regular cookies).

"Thank you. That is very thoughtful," Mrs. Holmes replied. She brushed her red hair from her forehead, then turned to Shelby. "Now, Shelby, you will have fruit for dessert tonight. No exceptions."

Uh-oh. I didn't want Dad to have to witness one of Shelby's infamous meltdowns.

But Shelby simply smiled. "That is fine, Mother."

Ah. What was going on? I mean, besides the fact that Shelby had inhaled an entire large sugar-filled pizza two hours ago?

Dad made small talk with Shelby's parents, while I sat down next to her. "Is it actually possible?"

"Is what possible?" she replied with a sniff.

I laughed. "That you're going to pass up a Levain cookie?" They were ginormous and gooey. And might be Shelby's favorite thing ever. Even I think they're pretty awesome, and I'm not someone who craves sweets.

"Please, Watson, I know where my mom will hide the leftovers."

"You do?"

"Of course. I'm fully versed on the best place to hide something."

"Where?"

"My parents have been doing regular searches of my backpack and room to make sure I'm not hiding any candy."

But Shelby had been hiding candy. A ton. So where was she putting it?

She handed me a book that was on the coffee table. "It's best to hide things in plain sight."

I opened the book and found the inside pages had been carved out, revealing a secret hiding place where Shelby currently had five candy bars stashed. I quickly shut the book before we were caught.

Shelby placed it back on the table, right in the middle of the room for all to see.

Okay, that was pretty smart. (Of course it was, it's *Shelby*!)

"Normally, if someone doesn't want you to find something, they'll put it in the last place you'd ever look. But that is precisely where you should look first," she stated.

"So where's your mom hiding sweets? Her underwear drawer?" I laughed some more. Man, I was pretty punchy on little sleep. Everything was hilarious to me.

Shelby grimaced. "No. An even worse place. Somewhere I would only dare venture under the most dire of circumstances."

"Where?" I asked. Where in their apartment could Shelby be almost scared of?

"The vegetable drawer, underneath the spinach." Shelby stuck her tongue out in disgust.

"Am I to presume by the look on your face you've tasted dinner?" Michael approached us slowly.

"No, I simply saw you coming," Shelby fired back to her brother.

He nodded at me. "John."

"Hey, Michael," I replied. When I first met Michael Holmes, I tried to treat him like anybody else. Be polite. Make small talk. But then I learned it was best to keep it short. And get out before he started asking impossible science questions.

Michael studied me with his normal bored look on his face. "I've been keeping up with your chronicles about my sister. The fiction you're able to spin with such uninspiring source material is quite a feat."

Wait. *Michael* was reading my journal? And I couldn't figure out if he was giving me a compliment or not. (Knowing Michael, he probably wasn't.)

"How brotherly of you to keep tabs on your sister," Shelby said with a glare.

"It is imperative for the brains of the family to look out for those with fewer talents."

Shelby smiled warmly at her brother. (This had to be a setup.) "You know what, my dear brother, you are quite amazing."

Michael looked pleased with himself. "Why thank yo—"

"Yes," Shelby cut him off. "It's truly amazing how one individual can be so daft."

I totally cracked up. I was feeling goofy. But come on, Michael. I'd only known Shelby for two months and I knew better. Michael couldn't be *that* smart if he kept challenging her.

Michael then turned to me. "I see we are under obligation to meet your father this evening."

"Oh, hey!" Dad came over and stuck out his hand. "You must be Michael. Martin Watson, nice to meet you."

Michael's lip curled under the strain while shaking Dad's hand. "Pleasure."

"I hear you're already in college. That's impressive!"

I tried to signal my dad to stop talking to Michael. I had warned him that he was a little prickly, even more so than Shelby.

"Well," Michael said, picking a piece of lint off his jacket, "what is truly extraordinary is why anybody would want to endure four years of high school."

"Ah," Dad replied as he rubbed his bald head, which I'd noticed was a tell for when he was at a loss for words.

I know Dad, I know.

A noise came from Dad's pocket. "Sorry!" he replied as he took out his phone, studied the screen, and then put it back in his pocket. "I thought I shut the ringer off."

I looked at Shelby in hopes that she could save us from Michael. (I realized how desperate I must be if I was looking to *Shelby* to make something less awkward.)

But Shelby was studying me with a worried look.

"What?" I asked her under my breath.

Her reply was to lightly pat me on the shoulder.

Oh no, this wasn't good. Why was Shelby feeling bad for me? The dinner couldn't be that disgusting. I actually liked the meals we had at the Holmeses'. Also, Shelby's parents always made her wear a dress, which annoyed her to no end, and that was pretty fun for me.

"I'm sorry you have to leave so soon, Mr. Watson," Shelby said quietly.

"What?" I said, louder this time. "Are we not staying for dinner?"

"Oh." Shelby shot Dad a disapproving look.

"He's not that fortunate to miss the brick that the parental units refer to as meatloaf," Michael replied. "Besides, his flight isn't until tomorrow."

I stood up. "WHAT?" I said even louder, hoping someone would finally answer me. Nothing seemed funny to me anymore, especially this. I didn't like that a conversation was happening around me, especially one concerning my dad. "Tomorrow's Thursday. He's not leaving until Sunday." I turned toward Dad, who couldn't look at me. "Right?"

"I wanted to tell you before we got here . . . ," he said in a small voice.

"Oh." I didn't hide my disappointment. Yeah, I knew he

was leaving eventually, but I wanted more time. "Why?" I asked a lot angrier than I meant to. But no, this wasn't fair. I had four more days with him. He was my dad—I should have a lot more time than that.

"Why don't we go into the hallway and talk?" Dad suggested.

The room was silent. Michael had opened a book, apparently not at all concerned with the fact that my life was falling apart in front of him. Shelby didn't move a muscle.

I jumped as Mr. and Mrs. Holmes came from the kitchen. "Dinner is served!"

Shelby stood up. "You two talk, I'll handle them." She grabbed Michael by the elbow and led him into the dining room.

"I'm really sorry, son," Dad said as he put his arm around me. "Something came up with work. They need me back in the office right away, so I was forced to change my plans. But I'll see you in a month for Thanksgiving."

"I had four more days," I whined. I even stamped my foot. I didn't care if I was acting like a spoiled kid. I wanted to spend time with my dad.

"I know, and again, I'm sorry. I'm not happy about it, either. I should've mentioned it the second I saw you, but I knew it would upset you."

Of course it was going to upset me!

But I couldn't say that. I didn't want my last night with Dad to be spent being angry, but I was. At the whole situation.

Dad pulled me in for a hug. "Listen, we'll have dinner and then you and I can go for a walk afterward. Just the two of us. And we can talk about what we'll do at Thanksgiving. Okay?"

He looked at me expectantly. I didn't want any of those things. What I wanted was for him to move here. For him and Mom to be able to be in the same room. None of this was my fault, but I was the one being punished for it.

But I knew I couldn't say anything. There was really only one answer I could give.

I swallowed the anger and frustration down. I forced a smile on my face.

"Okay, Dad."

CHAPTER
24

"MY BOY," DAD SAID AS HE PLACED HIS ARM AROUND MY shoulders as we walked around the neighborhood after dinner. "You know I'm so proud of you."

I simply shrugged in response. I wasn't in much of a mood for small talk. All through dinner I had to focus on not crying or throwing a fit over him leaving early. Now that I had the chance to tell him everything I felt, the words got caught in my throat.

"Listen." He stopped us in the middle of the sidewalk on Lenox. He moved in front of me so I had to look at him. "I know this has been hard on you, but you need to know it's been hard on me, too. I'm missing so much of your life. However much you miss me, I miss you that much and more. You're my son. I love you."

I looked down at the sidewalk. I wanted to believe him, but why was he leaving? Why couldn't he move here?

"Please look at me, John."

I clenched my jaw and looked up at my dad. There were tears welling in his eyes. Oh man, that almost broke me.

"I can't leave here thinking you're mad at me."

I shook my head. "I'm not mad." I was sad. I was angry at the divorce. But I could never be mad at him. He was my dad.

"It's not always going to be like this."

"Do you mean you're moving here?"

He sighed. "I don't know. I want to be closer, and I've talked to my superiors about maybe moving to the East Coast. But I won't know for a while. What I do know is that I want to see my boy smile before I have to get back on a plane. And know that you're also counting down the days until we see each other again."

"Twenty-eight," I said softly.

Dad leaned in. "What was that?"

I finally looked him in the eye. "There are twenty-eight days until I get on a plane for my visit."

Dad brightened up. "Is that a fact?"

Okay, so yeah, I totally have been crossing out the days on my calendar until I get to see him.

"It is." I couldn't help but smile. I was going to see him again in twenty-eight days.

Dad laughed. "Okay then, what do you want to do in

twenty-eight days?" He put his arm around me again as he continued to walk and talk about our next visit.

It still stung. But at least we had a future to plan.

There was a knock on my bedroom door an hour later.

Mom stuck her head in. "How are you doing?" she asked.

"Fine," I replied as I pulled up the covers around me. It wasn't even nine and I was already in bed.

She sat down next to me and rubbed my cheek with her thumb. "Oh, honey, I know you're upset, but you'll see him soon."

"Yeah." I did know that. And we already had a bunch of things Dad and I were going to do, but now that he was gone, it ended up hurting more.

"Why don't you and I do something special this weekend? Maybe go to Central Park or the Met. I think there's some kind of writers' exhibition at the Morgan Library."

"Okay." I gave Mom a hug. I didn't want her to think I wasn't happy to be spending time with her. She understood about my focus being on Dad (and the case) the last few days.

"Well, I came in to tell you that there's someone here to see you. You up for some company?" Mom stood and opened the door. I saw Shelby standing there with two napkins in her hand.

"Oh, hey," I said, a little embarrassed that Shelby was going to see me in my camouflage pajamas.

"Thanks, Dr. Watson," Shelby said as Mom closed the door behind us.

Shelby pulled my desk chair over toward me. "Here," she said as she handed me a napkin that had part of a chocolate chip cookie wrapped inside. "Your mom said it was okay."

It shouldn't come as a shock that I didn't have much of an appetite at dinner.

She then unfolded the other napkin that had the remaining part of the cookie.

"I wanted to—" Shelby began, but I had to cut her off.

"How did you know my dad's flight changed? And Michael?" But what I really wanted to know was why they knew before me. That was the part that upset me the most.

Shelby put the cookie down on my desk. "When he picked up his phone, I could see a flight notification pop up on his screen. You can't check into a flight until twenty-four hours before departure, so I knew he was leaving tomorrow. I presume Michael saw the exact same thing. I'm sorry that's how you found out. I should've deduced from your body language when you walked in that you were unaware."

I shrugged in response. I hadn't seen his phone, but I probably wouldn't have put it together even if I had. Since,

as Shelby has told me before, it was hard to see clearly if you had already made up your mind about something. And for me, I wouldn't have believed that my dad would leave early.

I was still in denial.

Shelby pursed her lips together and took a deep breath. She seemed unsure of herself, which wasn't like her. I almost wanted her to insult me or something to get my life back to normal. I mean, my life wasn't really normal anymore without Dad, but I had a new normal and I had to accept the fact that he wasn't going to be a big part of it.

"Okay, Watson, I want to tell you something." She got up and sat next to me on the bed, right where Mom had just been. "You know I can see things that others can't."

I nodded because well, *duh*.

"Your father really cares about you. In the time that I've been with the two of you, I've observed how he beams when you talk. How he gets sad when you discuss things he's missed, like your first day of school or when you were in the ambulance. But today, it didn't take a genius of my caliber to see how much it tore him apart that he had to leave. You need to know that your father loves you, and just because he isn't here all the time doesn't mean he cares less about you."

I was stunned. Yeah, Dad basically told me the same thing, but . . . I don't know. It was different hearing it from

Shelby. She didn't say things to make you feel better about yourself. She told you the truth. She told you what you needed to hear, and not what you wanted to hear.

I looked down at my hands. It was hard to look Shelby in the eyes. I didn't want to cry in front of her, but what she said meant a lot to me. "Thanks, Shelby."

"I'm simply stating facts," she replied as she got up. She began studying my room. "Could you be more of a male cliché?" she stated as she took in my basketball posters.

I let out a forced laugh as I took a bite of my cookie.

"Hey, Shelby," I said as she returned her attention to me. "You're a really good friend. And well, I just wanted you to know that."

"Thank you. And Watson"—she folded her arms—"I wanted you to know that . . . your pajamas are absolutely ridiculous."

Well, with that burn it seemed my life had returned to its new normal.

And, even though I was still sad, I couldn't be more grateful for it and for Shelby.

~·CHAPTER·~
25

JUST YESTERDAY, I WANTED THIS CASE TO BE OVER.

But now I was happy for the distraction.

You didn't need to be a Shelby Holmes to know what I didn't want to think about.

At the skating rink the next morning, I walked over to the outskirts of the rink. I didn't even have a chance to sit down before Tatiana skated toward me.

"Do you have report?" she asked.

"We should wait for Shelby," I replied. Shelby was usually out before me, but I simply threw my bag in the boys' locker room before coming out. I didn't even bother to lock it up. I figured if something happened to me then we would know for sure it was Douglas. Maybe he'd leave me a note. Maybe he'd try to steal something. (I was really hoping he'd steal my homework or that awful outfit Shelby asked me to carry "just in case." I didn't want to know in which circumstances that sparkly monstrosity would be needed.)

I also didn't know what to say to Tatiana. Yesterday we

thought it was either Aisha or Douglas—and all signs pointed to Aisha. But now it could be Douglas, Sergi, Belle, or Belle's mom. Even though Belle's mom said she didn't understand the cipher, I didn't trust her. I wasn't about to be the one to tell Tatiana that we were further away from finding the person than ever.

Oh, and also, I had no idea *how* we were going to figure out who was sending the messages. And I really didn't want to have to get here even earlier to try to catch the person as they left the cipher, but I wasn't sure we had any other options.

I looked around the two rinks. Sergi was busy with Belle, Douglas, and Aisha skating around. Belle's mom was in her usual hovering position. Jordan was stretching off to the side of Tatiana's rink. She didn't seem especially bothered.

"Do you have a new cipher for us?" I asked.

Tatiana shook her head. "No."

"Really?" I was concerned. We didn't have one yesterday and look what happened. Someone tampered with Jordan's water. What would be next?

Tatiana sighed. "I thought you would know by now. Regionals in two days." She appeared annoyed.

I didn't blame her. I was annoyed we hadn't figured this out yet.

"We'll get whoever is behind this," I replied confidently, even though I wasn't so sure.

Tatiana skated off without another word. I bent over to

tie my skates, dreading the fact that we were going to have to skate since we didn't have a cipher to decode. I wasn't in the mood to hear Belle's mom tell us how useless we were.

I tied my second skate and when I looked up, something on the side of the rink caught my eye. It couldn't possibly be . . .

I took a couple steps and then knelt beside the gate to Tatiana's rink. There it was. Another message written on the paneling:

Tatiana and Jordan must've not seen it. I reached inside my skate to produce the key code to the cipher. (Shelby wasn't the only person who could use it as storage!) I didn't have anything to write on, so I tried to do it in my head.

The first word had two letters we hadn't gotten yet. I looked back to the girls' locker room, willing Shelby to come out to help me. The first word was WAT--. Okay, maybe I could figure it out using the rest of the words.

Second word was *out*. Okay, so it was WAT-- OUT. We still didn't have the letters for *B*, *C*, *H*—then it hit me.

WATCH OUT

While I should've been happy the bully wasn't calling Jordan any names, I was worried. They had moved on to threats.

But *what* was Jordan supposed to watch out for?

And maybe it was something to help us. Something that would lead us to the culprit! Maybe this was the break we'd been looking for!

I quickly decoded the third word and it was . . . *Nancy*?

WATCH OUT NANCY

Nancy? Who was Nancy?

Could it be that these messages were never intended for Jordan and they were for another girl named Nancy?

That would just be the icing on this mess of a case.

"What are you doing?" Shelby asked as she walked over, her skates already on.

"There's a message," I said as I guided Shelby away from the code not to draw attention to us. The person who left it was in the room. We didn't want them to know that we were onto him or her.

Shelby started stretching. "What does it say?"

"Watch out, Nancy," I replied as I bent over to stretch out my legs.

"Who's Nancy?"

I didn't know if I should be worried or relieved that Shelby didn't know, either. We were both clueless.

(Yeah, I should've been worried.)

Wait a second. The name Nancy was familiar. Not from the rink, but there was a skater named Nancy.

It was the story my dad told me. I'd been trying to push away all my memories of his visit since it was too hard to think about what I had before he abruptly left. But this was important. He told me about those two skaters. The ones who made the news all those years ago.

I sucked in my breath.

"What is it, Watson?" Shelby asked, a concerned look on her face.

"It's Jordan."

"Jordan is Nancy. That doesn't make sense."

"No." I looked over at Jordan as she started skating. "Jordan's in real danger."

$\backsim$ CHAPTER $\backsim$
26

MY EYES SCANNED THE RINK, WONDERING IF SOMEONE WAS lurking in the shadows preparing to hit Jordan on the knee.

No. Nobody would do that when we were all out here together.

But maybe they were going to do something else. I thought about what Jordan did to Aisha. (Allegedly.) Maybe they were going to tamper with something like her shoelaces.

Jordan kept skating. She was building momentum. That meant she was getting ready to jump.

What would happen if she jumped and her shoelace broke?

Before I realized what I was doing, I threw open the door to the rink and skated toward her.

"Stop!" I called out.

Jordan ignored me and continued to pick up speed.

"STOP!" I waved my hands at her, but in my rush, I tripped and fell flat on the ice.

Tatiana came skating over with Jordan behind her. "What is going on?" Tatiana demanded. "You interrupt practice."

"Yes, I'd also like to inquire into your behavior, Watson," Shelby commented as she skated behind me.

I got up from the ice. Jordan, Tatiana, and Shelby were standing in front of me, all waiting impatiently.

One glance at the other rink showed that everybody over there was now focused on me as well.

Awesome.

I had to remind myself I was still undercover as far as Sergi, Douglas, Belle, and her mom were concerned. You know, our suspects.

"There was another message today. You didn't see it," I said, surprised how out of breath I was from my quick sprint . . . and subsequent fall. "I think someone is going to mess with your skates."

"What exactly did message say?" Tatiana asked.

"Watch out, Nancy."

"Who is—" Jordan began to ask before her eyes got wide. "Oh. But there's nothing wrong with my skates."

She moved around a little. It seemed fine. But she hadn't really done anything difficult yet.

"Look, I'm okay," Jordan said. "I'll be extra careful when I leave the rink. Now, can you please clear the way so I can skate."

"Okay, okay." I skated over to her with only a little wobble. "Can you please just take your skates off so we can get a good look? Then I'll leave you alone." I'd feel awful if anything happened to Jordan.

"That's not necessary. See?" Jordan said as she took her left foot and slammed the toe pick down. Little flakes of ice came up on contact. She picked up her right foot. "Like I said, everything is—" As soon as the front half of her blade came in contact with the ice, it came undone from her boot.

It left a tiny dent in the middle of the rink.

Oh, wow. I was right. *I WAS RIGHT!*

But I couldn't feel that great about it because, well, yikes.

"What is going on?" Sergi shouted over the plastic partition that separated the two rinks.

"Mind own business!" Tatiana replied.

The four of us looked down at Jordan's broken skate.

Her right skate. The one that she used for the majority of her jumps.

This was getting serious.

And we were running out of time.

Shelby bent down, pretending to retie her skate, but instead inspected Jordan's boot. "Someone must've loosened the screws. The skating you've done has continued to dislodge them. I don't want to think what would've happened if you attempted a Lutz on this skate."

I didn't, either. Jordan could've really gotten hurt.

"Excellent job, Watson," Shelby remarked with a nod of respect.

I felt my chest swell, until I looked over at Jordan and saw the blood draining from her face.

"What are we going to do?" Jordan asked. I think it had finally settled in that there was a real problem. And it wasn't just messing with her mind. This person was taking it a step further. A dangerous step further.

"We need a team meeting," Shelby said as she got back up.

We made our way off the ice. Jordan held on to Tatiana's arm as she skated on her one good skate.

"What is going on?" Mrs. Booth approached us. "What happened to Jordan's skate? And are you two really skaters? Because Julian can hardly stay on his feet."

Yeah, like I needed her to tell me that.

"Yes, we are skaters," Shelby replied with a huff. (And conveniently not answering the question about Jordan's skate, although maybe Mrs. Booth knew exactly what happened and was playing coy.) Shelby blocked Mrs. Booth while Jordan hobbled to Tatiana's office. "I'm seriously contemplating making a switch to a better partner. Isn't that something Douglas has done . . . more than once?" Shelby raised her eyebrow at Mrs. Booth.

Well, that quieted her up.

Shelby and I quickly followed Jordan and Tatiana to the office. Once the door was closed behind us, Shelby took over.

"Enough is enough. The time has come for us to meet the culprit face-to-face."

CHAPTER 27

IT WAS TRUE: MIRACLES COULD HAPPEN.

"Is this seat taken?"

Our Thursday lunchtime conversation stopped as the guys and I looked up and saw Shelby with her lunch bag.

She plopped down next to me before we could reply. "We have work to do."

"Oh," Jason said as he rubbed his hands together. "This is going to be so good. I've been waiting to see you guys in action."

Shelby replied by looking at Jason blankly.

"Ah, Shelby, you know Jason." I introduced her even though she'd been going to the Academy longer than me.

"I am already acquainted with everybody," she stated as she waved around the table dismissively.

The guys all stared at her. And yeah, practically the rest of the cafeteria was watching. Shelby Holmes didn't eat lunch with other people.

Nobody said anything. A quiet lull took over the room.

(Okay, as much as I wanted Shelby to join us for lunch, I didn't realize how uncomfortable it would be. Which was a little foolish of me because it was Shelby Holmes in a normal friend environment. OF COURSE it would be uncomfortable.)

Bryant glared at Shelby. "So, as I was saying—"

"What's that?" John Wu asked as Shelby took out the cipher.

"Those are cool symbols," Carlos said as he studied them. "Very caveman. Me like ham." He took a big bite of his sandwich.

Bryant cleared his throat loudly. "Can we get back to—"

"Is that the code?" John asked. He leaned in closer to look at the cipher. "That is so cool. How did you break it?"

"The way you handle any difficult puzzle, piece by piece," Shelby replied.

"Oh, hey, I got this for you." John reached into his bag and gave Shelby a bag of mini Snickers. "The Halloween candy is out. I know it's tiny bars, but thought you'd appreciate the quantity."

Shelby perked up as she ripped open the bag. "I do. Smart thinking."

"Nice!" John held out his fist for a bump. Shelby studied his hand for a second before going back to eating her candy.

(I mean, really, they should all know better at this point.)

"So are we all just going to gush over her or can we talk about something else?" Bryant sulked.

"Dude, it's cool," Jason replied as he pulled his locs back. "We've got a guest and she's brought part of her case. I've been dying to hear about this."

"A guest? A GUEST?" Bryant stood up.

I didn't realize how much he really didn't like Shelby. I knew he found her annoying and smug and his competition . . . But I didn't realize he was going to be so rude in front of her.

"Nobody is making you stay," Shelby replied with a sniff. Although I should've called it that Shelby wouldn't have a problem putting Bryant in his place.

"Shelby," I warned her. I didn't want my friends to fight. "Come on, Bryant. Sit down. Shelby and I have a case to work on. We can move to another table."

"NO!" Jason, Carlos, and John all said at once.

"Well, I know where I'm not wanted," Bryant snapped before grabbing his lunch and leaving the table.

"Bryant," I called after him, but he walked out of the cafeteria without even a glance over his shoulder.

"He'll calm down," Jason said as he got up. "I'll go talk to him."

"Yeah. Me too," I seconded. I didn't want Bryant to be

mad at us, but we only had a day left to get to the bottom of this case. Who knew what would happen if Jordan competed in regionals without knowing who was behind this.

"You stay. Listen, good luck with your case, I can't wait to read all about it," Jason said before going after Bryant.

"Are all friendships this dramatic?" Shelby asked with a roll of her eyes. "Boys."

Oh, yeah, boys were the ones who were dramatic. Right. If Shelby had any girlfriends she would see that boys were a cakewalk. Or, you know, she could try to be her own friend for a day.

Girls.

"This thing is really cool," Carlos said. He was doodling in his sketchbook. "There are little differences, but it's pretty intricate. I don't know what I'm saying right now, but it looks good. Like all my work." He reached out his hand for John to high-five, which he did as he shook his head.

Shelby studied his ciphers. "It looks exactly like the code that person has been leaving behind. Every line and curve."

"Oh, sorry." Carlos gulped nervously. "I can stop. Or do it different."

"No," Shelby said. She then closed her eyes.

Carlos and John looked around at me for an answer to what she was doing. I wasn't sure exactly what she was thinking, but I knew she did that when she was trying to figure something out.

John leaned toward us. "I often do that before I have to perform a big scene," he whispered. "I train and rehearse, but as the great Stella Adler said, 'The most important thing the actor has to work on is his mind.'"

"Uh-huh," I replied. *Great.* Usually John would do some Shakespeare quote or something, but now he was quoting random people? Who was Stella Adler? I blame Shelby. They've been spending too much time together. Why couldn't his sense of humor rub off on *her*?

Shelby opened her eyes and we all quieted down. She turned to Carlos, who immediately stopped sketching. "Ah, here," he said as he gave her the cipher back.

Shelby then turned to me. "Sergi has given his team tomorrow morning off so they can have a good night's rest the day before regionals. But they do have practice this evening. So far this has been a one-sided conversation. We are going to finally reply to this knave."

Did this mean that we got tomorrow morning off as well? I couldn't believe I would actually look forward to sleeping in until seven. Seven was late now! (This case had completely ruined me.)

"And you." She pointed to Carlos who looked like he was going to be sick. "I need you to write this down."

He looked back and forth at the piece of paper she gave him and the code. "You . . . You want *my* help?"

"Well, not if you're going to make a big deal of it," Shelby said in a huff as she reached for the code.

"No! I'll do it!" Carlos lit up.

I patted him on the back. It was always nice when Shelby admitted, even though she didn't necessarily *say* it, that you had skills that were better than hers. Carlos was a great artist. He could make the code look exactly the way Shelby wanted it to.

First, John Wu. Now, Carlos.

Maybe Shelby would eventually be in with the guys. We could all hang out. They could help us from time to time. Although who was I kidding? Bryant would never agree to that.

"Okay, Watson," Shelby said as a smirk crossed her face. "It's time we set our trap."

CHAPTER 28

"I DON'T LIKE THIS AT ALL." TATIANA PACED THE SMALL AREA to the side of the rink at six o'clock the following morning.

That's right: six in the morning. So yeah, no sleeping in for me.

Jordan skated to the center of the rink where the only lights were illuminated. Sergi's rink and the outskirts were completely dark.

"You need to stay down," Shelby said as she grabbed Tatiana by the arm and pulled her to a squatted position. "We can't risk being seen and tipping off the culprit that we're here. They are under the impression that they're only meeting Jordan here to talk."

The rink was eerily quiet. Usually it was noisy with the sounds of skates, music, and the coaches (and Belle's mom) shouting out orders. But now I could only hear my own breath.

"Breathe through your nose, Watson," Shelby scolded.

"What exactly did note say?" Tatiana asked before

Shelby cut her off with a look. It was too dark for me to see Shelby's exact expression, but it was Shelby, so most likely it was a displeased one.

Yesterday after school, we snuck in before their evening practice and left a note taped to Sergi's office wall: *You win. Meet me on the ice. Six a.m. Unless scared.*

Shelby thought it would be best not only to make the person think that Jordan was giving up skating, but to taunt them into coming. They kept saying mean things about Jordan, so it was time the favor was somewhat returned.

Jordan was alone on center ice, her arms folded. She tried to pretend she wasn't scared, but her body language betrayed her: rapid blinking and cracking of knuckles. Shelby originally wanted to put a wig on and pretend to be Jordan, but Jordan had about eight inches on Shelby in height and muscular legs. Shelby's skinny legs looked like my arms.

We waited in silence. Maybe the person didn't see the note? Maybe they wouldn't come?

But the question that kept popping into my head was the most important one: Who did it? Who was this person?

My money was on Douglas. Or Sergi. They had the most to gain if Jordan didn't compete. Douglas would prove that Jordan was better off with him, while Sergi would get revenge on Tatiana and help his skater, Aisha, win.

Hmmm. The scale was currently tipping toward Sergi.

Plus, we didn't really know much about Sergi.

Although let's be honest: it seemed to tip in different directions every few minutes. But for now, Sergi. Yes, definitely Sergi.

Or Douglas.

The door to the rink opened with a creak. We heard the sound of footsteps.

Someone was here.

Jordan turned toward the door. She had been instructed not to leave the center, no matter what. We were only twenty feet away from the entrance so we could get to the person before they could do anything to Jordan.

Unless they had skates on and jumped into the rink before we could stop them. But Jordan was fast on her skates.

(Maybe this was a bad plan.)

A voice cut through the quiet. "So you wanted to meet."

It was a woman's voice. A deep voice. I didn't recognize it.

Maybe it was Belle's mom?

"Why don't you show your face?" Jordan said.

"I'm not stupid," the voice replied.

You know, the voice sounded strained. Like the woman was trying to mask her voice. That was why she wasn't coming forward into the light. I maneuvered slightly to see if I could get a look. She was wearing a hoodie that was covering her face. But she was petite. Although every figure skater seemed to be tiny.

My stomach plunged. What if it *was* Aisha? If she was

diabolical enough to be doing this, she would've known to hide her handwriting in the cipher she sent me. And she did have the most to lose.

Oh, Watson, you're such a fool.

Jordan started skating in a small circle. "I'm not surprised you're a coward. You had to hide behind a code instead of saying something to my face." Jordan kept to the script that Shelby had written for her in an effort to draw the person out. Because, of course, Shelby foresaw that we might be in the exact scenario we were in.

John Wu even helped Shelby with the script. They took inspiration from some play. I had to go in and tone it down a bit as one of their suggested lines was, "Alas, I thought I knew thee well." (Why I had to tell them no normal person talked like that was beyond me.)

I turned to look at Shelby but she was gone. Like she vanished. Tatiana shrugged her shoulders in response. Where did she go?

Suddenly the main lights flooded the entire rink. I had to shield my eyes for a second to get them adjusted to the bright light. I looked over at the woman who was doing the same thing. Then she put her arms down, and I got a good look at her face.

It wasn't Aisha.

It wasn't Belle's mom.

It was Belle.

CHAPTER
29

BELLE?!?!

Sure, we knew she had the code, but she was so sweet and quiet.

Shelby stepped behind Belle and blocked her exit. "Start talking."

Belle blinked a few times. "Oh, hello." She returned her voice to its natural high tone. "I'm simply here for practice. How are you, Roberta? You look . . . different today."

Shelby's hair was its usual mess and she was wearing her Academy polo and baggy jeans. She didn't feel the need to play the part anymore. "That's because this is the real me. And my name isn't Roberta, it's Shelby Holmes. *Detective* Shelby Holmes."

Belle's eyes got wide, but it wasn't from shock. She was playing up the whole innocent bit. I wasn't buying it. "A detective? Oh my goodness, what on earth is going on? You mean you and Julian aren't skaters?"

Oh, *come on.* Nobody could really believe that Shelby and

I were skaters. I guess Belle was a good actress. Because she was playing the naive part really well.

Jordan skated over to the side. Tatiana and I walked toward Belle and Shelby.

"Good morning," Belle replied to us in her usual sunny way, as she removed her hood. "Everybody ready for a great skate today?"

Shelby started circling Belle. "You're here for practice?"

"Why, of course. Sergi said it was optional, but I wanted to get in another skate before tomorrow."

"Then where is Sergi? Or Douglas?"

"I'm here by myself. I have a few elements to work on."

Shelby stopped in front of Belle, an impatient expression on her face. "And then where, pray tell, are your skates?"

"Oh, I—I—" Belle stuttered. She took a deep breath and continued, "I have them in the locker room. I came out here to stretch first."

Jordan opened up the gate to the rink and stalked over to Belle. "How could you do this to me? We know it was you who was sending me those notes. And put something in my water. *And* messed up my skates. Why? WHY?"

Yeah, *WHY*?

"I've been nothing but nice and supportive to you," Jordan continued. "When you first came here, I took you out and told you all about being Douglas's partner and working with Sergi. I was helping you and *this* is how you repay me?"

Belle was frozen for a moment before her innocent expression turned to hate. "Oh yes, you are just SO perfect. Perfect Jordan who can skate perfect and was the perfect partner!" She stomped her foot. "I'm so sick of hearing about you!"

Okay, Belle was not this sweet and nice person. She was angry. And a little scary.

Tatiana stepped forward. "Now, Belle—"

"NO!" Belle screamed. "I never get to talk. My mom talks over me all the time. Belle, do this. Belle, wear that.

Belle, change your hair so you can look just like Jordan. Well, not anymore. I'm going to talk and you can't shut me up."

"So talk," Shelby said. She looked like she was enjoying this. I guess it was good we didn't have to interrogate her or anything because she was telling us all we needed to know.

"I just had it. All day at practice I hear from Sergi and Douglas about how *Jordan* used to do something and how I needed to be more like *Jordan*. And then at home Mom just keeps going on and on about how perfect *Jordan* was at practice that day." She turned toward Jordan. "All I wanted was to skate without you being around. To be Belle and not simply a replacement for you. One that was never going to be good enough. I thought if I sent you some notes you'd go away for a bit. Or change your practice times. I didn't want to hurt you, but you weren't getting the hints. I've always done what's right and what's expected of me. I'm done. DONE. What about what I want? Huh?"

Tatiana looked sad. "Do you not want to skate?"

"No," Shelby replied. "She wants to be the best."

"And what's wrong with that?" Belle snapped.

"How dare you?" Jordan stepped forward, but I held my arm out to block her. Which wasn't easy, because she was strong. "You tried to ruin me."

"You look fine to me," Belle replied with a smirk. "Too bad."

"Okay, okay," Shelby said as she stepped between them. "Jordan, you can go back to skating and get ready for tomorrow. I'll examine your equipment to confirm it's safe. You won't be getting any more notes. Focus on tomorrow."

"I'm going to win." Jordan narrowed her eyes at Belle. "Pity I can't say the same for Douglas. He's had such a difficult time finding a competent partner."

With that she flipped her ponytail and went back to the skating rink with Tatiana behind her.

Belle looked blankly at Shelby. "So what now? Are you going to tell the US Figure Skating Association?"

"Worse," Shelby replied.

For the first time since we caught her, Belle looked worried.

I would be, too. What was worse than letting the skating authorities know about this?

"You can come out now," Shelby shouted.

"You called the cops!" Belle shrieked.

Shelby laughed. "What did I tell you? Worse."

Worse than the cops?

I was confused until I saw who Shelby was talking to.

Stepping out from behind the benches was Belle's mom.

Uh-oh.

·CHAPTER·
30

HOLD UP.

Just.

Hold.

Up.

What was Mrs. Booth doing here?

Before I could ask Shelby, Mrs. Booth marched over to her daughter. Her face was bright red. "I can't believe this, Belle. How could you do this to another person? You've ruined everything we've worked so hard for!"

"But you never listen to me!" Belle shouted.

Mrs. Booth looked like steam was about to come out of her ears. "Well, your wish is granted. We're going to your father's office right now to have a nice long conversation about this."

"But—"

"Not another word until we see your father," Belle's mom said in a tone that I don't think anybody would mess with. "Now get in the car."

Belle stomped off.

Shelby was not exaggerating when she said Mrs. Booth was worse than the cops and figure skating officials.

I would not want to be Belle right now. Not like she didn't deserve it.

Mrs. Booth took a look at us, then a deep breath. "I knew you weren't skaters. But I guess I have no choice but to thank you, Shelby and John. If you'll excuse me, I have a troubled daughter to deal with." She exited the rink shaking her head.

Wait a second. Mrs. Booth knew our names. Our real names. She was here. Which meant . . .

"Shelby, did you know it was Belle who was sending the notes?"

"Of course I did."

OF COURSE SHE DID.

"But how? When?" And, you know, *why didn't she tell me*?!?!

"Belle had always been a suspect, but things started adding up in the last two days. You already had the benefit of hearing her motives directly from Belle. When she was forced to wear the wig, I began to pay more attention to her. Her attitude. Her movements, especially whenever anybody mentioned Jordan's name. We knew she had the code. But she was my lead suspect since Wednesday."

"Wednesday?"

"Yes, when the water was tampered with."

"How?" There weren't any clues except that one fiber from a black glove. "Belle wasn't wearing a black glove that day." I should know, I was the one who checked.

"She was wearing a yellow and white snowflake glove made of alpaca. The glove's wrist, which you couldn't properly see from the rink, was bordered with a dark gray, almost black, pattern. Which matched the fiber from the one I found on Jordan's bottle."

"Then how did *you* see it? And get a fiber?"

"I told her I admired her gloves and asked to try them on." Shelby started walking toward the exit. "That was also when I confirmed she was left-handed."

"Where was I?" I followed her. How did I miss this?

Shelby shrugged. "I can't be held accountable for your whereabouts at all times. You were around, probably simply not paying proper attention."

Unbelievable. Actually, no. It was believable because it was Shelby.

"Details, Watson. Details."

Ugh. I guess she had me. I didn't notice it. At all.

"Well, it would've been nice if you could've filled me in!" I argued.

Shelby paused before she opened the main exit to the Sky Rink. "But, what would've been the fun in that?"

Shelby and I really needed to have a talk about what the word *fun* means.

"Besides, you've contributed in a few significant ways to this case," Shelby admitted with a light tap on my back. "You should feel quite pleased with yourself for preventing Jordan from getting injured yesterday. Without your astute observation, she might not have been in any condition to compete tomorrow. Leaving this entire investigation for naught."

You know what, I was proud of that. It *was* a big deal. I was getting better with each case. So I didn't know it was Belle, but I probably would've eventually gotten there if, you know, my partner would've shared all the facts with me.

"We have an hour before we have to head to school." Shelby clapped her hands together excitedly. "Now let's go to Doughnut Plant to celebrate another successful client!"

I shook my head as I followed Shelby out since she'd be the only one eating doughnuts, but who was I to argue?

Another case solved for Holmes and Watson.

CHAPTER
31

OKAY. *OKAY.* I'LL ADMIT IT: FIGURE SKATING IS A REAL sport.

However, I'm happy to report that John Watson—or Julian Law—is retired from figure skating.

Jordan was currently skating her free skate program at regionals. She was the last one to perform. Aisha had just finished her program that looked perfect to me and was currently in first place.

Jordan did a jump and landed it perfectly.

"That's the best triple flip I've seen from her," I remarked to Shelby.

Whoa. WHAT WAS I EVEN TALKING ABOUT?

My phone buzzed in my pocket. It was Dad asking who won.

The good news on the Dad front was that I was hearing from him more now since he'd been back in Kentucky. Plus, it was nice that he knew the people who I talked about, but still. It wasn't the same. I had to realize it never would be.

And I guess I had to get used to that.

I decided to focus on the positive. Shelby and I had solved another case. Belle did skate with Douglas today because it wouldn't have been fair to Douglas to leave him without a partner. Although Mrs. Booth was putting Belle in therapy so she could work on her "competitive issues."

Yeah, that might've been an understatement. And honestly, I don't think therapy would hurt Mrs. Booth, either.

But the coolest part was that Shelby and I were going to be key witnesses in the US Figure Skating Association investigation against Belle since Jordan and Tatiana weren't going to let it slide.

John Watson: star witness, detective, retired skater.

Tatiana was so happy we figured it out, Shelby was rewarded with a duffel bag full of candy that should last her a month.

And well, I was rewarded, too.

I grasped the new leather journal Tatiana gave me. It was Shelby's suggestion. She realized that all-candy rewards weren't really fair to me. So maybe Shelby learned a little something about teamwork with this case. Tatiana also included a twenty-dollar bill inside the journal, which I used to take Bryant out for some pizza to smooth things over.

We're good. For now. Not sure what's going to happen if we need the guys to help us again. But I have to admit that it was cool to get them involved, even if it made Bryant mad.

"Jordan's doing well," Shelby said as she took a bite of five Twizzlers at once.

(Okay, so that bag was only lasting her a week.)

Jordan finished with a superfast spin and the audience jumped to their feet clapping for her. She cracked the tiniest of smiles as she skated off to Tatiana.

"I wonder who's going to win," I said.

(And yes, I was rooting for Aisha.

I mean, could you blame me?)

Shelby glanced at her phone and then stood up. "Come along, Watson."

"But, Shelby," I protested, "we have to wait for the results!"

"No time."

No time? We'd know in two minutes who won. We'd spent all week with these people. I was invested!

What on earth—

But I already knew. And as much as I wanted to see the end of the competition, there was only one thing that would drag Shelby away.

I couldn't wait to hear her say it. It never got old.

"We've got another case to solve."

ACKNOWLEDGMENTS

I am so incredibly grateful to the gold-medal team at Bloomsbury for all their work on this series. Huge thanks to my editor, Hali Baumstein, for *not* making me cry with her very thoughtful editor letter (hey, there's a first time for everything!). I'm so appreciative Jeanette Levy and Donna Mark were accommodating when I told them this book featured a cipher and then remarked, "So, good luck with that!" Can I consider myself an artist now? (Better to not answer that.) Bags and bags of candy to the whole team: Diane Aronson, Erica Barmash, Bethany Buck, Cristina Gilbert, Melissa Kavonic, Cindy Loh, Lizzy Mason, Patricia McHugh, Linda Minton, Brittany Mitchell, Emily Ritter, and Sarah Shumway. And cheers to the team in the UK: Nicholas Church, Zoe Griffiths, Callum Kenny, Anna de Lacey, Andrea Kearney, and Lizz Skelly.

I'm so lucky to have Erwin Madrid bring Shelby and Watson to life. Especially as my ciphers showed, I am NOT an artist.

Shelby would still be an idea in my head if it weren't for my agent's encouragement. Thank you, Erin Malone and the entire team at WME, especially Laura Bonner.

Writing is a very solitary career, so I'm grateful to all my fellow middle-grade author friends who have been so supportive, especially Jen Calonita, Stuart Gibbs, Varian Johnson, and Sarah Mlynowski.

I didn't just watch *The Cutting Edge* on repeat to write this book. Thank you to Annabelle Collins for answering my questions about competitive figure skating. And, Kirk Benshoff, as always for keeping my website as sparkly as a figure skating outfit.

An author is nothing without readers. So thank you, thank you, THANK YOU to every reader who has picked up my book and every librarian, teacher, or bookseller who has placed my book into a reader's hand. Shelby and Watson are up for more adventures if you guys are!

One final note: Being a detective means you have to be very clear about the facts, but writing a detective book sometimes means you use your artistic license to fudge a few facts. In reality, there's a lobby that separates the two skating rinks at Chelsea Piers. I put them together in this book to force the suspects to all be in one room. It made, in my opinion, for a better read. But there's no doubt that Shelby would definitely not approve. AT ALL. Oh well!